ARTEMIS FOWL

Eoin Colfer

VIKING

VIKING

Published by the Penguin Group
Penguin Books Ltd, 27 Wrights Lane, London W8 5TZ, England
Penguin Putnam Inc., 375 Hudson Street, New York, New York 10014, USA
Penguin Books Australia Ltd, Ringwood, Victoria, Australia
Penguin Books Canada Ltd, 10 Alcorn Avenue, Toronto, Ontario, Canada M4V 3B2
Penguin Books India (P) Ltd, 11 Community Centre, Panchsheel Park, New Delhi – 110 017, India
Penguin Books (NZ) Ltd, Cnr Rosedale and Airborne Roads, Albany, Auckland, New Zealand
Penguin Books (South Africa) (Pty) Ltd, 5 Watkins Street, Denver Ext 4, Johannesburg 2094,
South Africa

On the World Wide Web at: www.penguin.com

Penguin Books Ltd, Registered Offices: Harmondsworth, Middlesex, England

First published 2001
2

Set in 13.5/16.3pt Perpetua

Made and printed in England by Clays Ltd, St Ives plc

British Library Cataloguing in Publication Data
A CIP catalogue record for this book is available from the British Library

ISBN 0–670–91183–6

ARTEMIS
FOWL

For Jackie

COΠTEΠTS

PROLOGUE

How does one describe Artemis Fowl? Various psychiatrists have tried and failed. The main problem is Artemis's own intelligence. He bamboozles every test thrown at him. He has puzzled the greatest medical minds and sent many of them gibbering to their own hospitals.

There is no doubt that Artemis is a child prodigy. But why does someone of such brilliance dedicate himself to criminal activities? This is a question that can be answered by only one person. And he delights in not talking.

Perhaps the best way to create an accurate picture of Artemis is to tell the by now famous account of his first villainous venture. I have put together this report from first-hand interviews with the victims, and as the tale unfolds you will realize that this was not easy.

The story began several years ago at the dawn of

the twenty-first century. Artemis Fowl had devised a plan to restore his family's fortune. A plan that could topple civilizations and plunge the planet into a cross-species war.

He was twelve years old at the time ...

CHAPTER I: **THE BOOK**

 HO Chi Minh City in the summer. Sweltering by anyone's standards. Needless to say, Artemis Fowl would not have been willing to put up with such discomfort if something extremely important had not been at stake. Important to the plan.

Sun did not suit Artemis. He did not look well in it. Long hours indoors in front of the monitor had bleached the glow from his skin. He was white as a vampire and almost as testy in the light of day.

'I hope this isn't another wild-goose chase, Butler,' he said, his voice soft and clipped. 'Especially after Cairo.'

It was a gentle rebuke. They had travelled to Egypt on the word of Butler's informant.

'No, sir. I'm certain this time. Nguyen is a good man.'

'Hmm,' droned Artemis, unconvinced.

Passers-by would have been amazed to hear the large Eurasian refer to the boy as *sir*. This was, after all, the third millennium. But this was no ordinary relationship, and these were no ordinary tourists.

They were sitting outside a kerbside cafe on Dong Khai Street, watching the local teenagers circle the square on mopeds.

Nguyen was late, and the pathetic patch of shade provided by the umbrella was doing little to improve Artemis's mood. But this was just his daily pessimism. Beneath the sulk was a spark of hope. Could this trip actually yield results? Would they find the Book? It was too much to hope for.

A waiter scurried to their table.

'More tea, sirs?' he asked, head bobbing furiously.

Artemis sighed. 'Spare me the theatrics and sit down.'

The waiter turned instinctively to Butler, who was, after all, the adult.

'But, sir, I am the waiter.'

Artemis tapped the table for attention.

'You are wearing handmade loafers, a silk shirt and three gold signet rings. Your English has a tinge of Oxford about it and your nails have the soft sheen of the recently manicured. You are not a waiter. You are our contact, Nguyen Xuan, and you have adopted this pathetic disguise to discreetly check for weaponry.'

Nguyen's shoulders sagged. 'It is true. Amazing.'

'Hardly. A ragged apron does not a waiter make.'

Nguyen sat, pouring some mint tea into a tiny china cup.

'Let me fill you in on the weapons status,' continued Artemis. 'I am unarmed. But Butler here, my … ah … butler, has a Sig Sauer in his shoulder holster, two shrike throwing knives in his boots, a derringer two-shot up his sleeve, garrotte wire in his watch and three stun grenades concealed in various pockets. Anything else, Butler?'

'The cosh, sir.'

'Oh yes. A good old ball-bearing cosh stuffed down his shirt.'

Nguyen brought the cup trembling to his lips.

'Don't be alarmed, Mister Xuan,' smiled Artemis. 'The weapons will not be used on you.'

Nguyen didn't seem reassured.

'No,' continued Artemis. 'Butler could kill you a hundred different ways without the use of his armoury. Though I'm sure one would be quite sufficient.'

Nguyen was by now thoroughly spooked. Artemis generally had that effect on people. A pale adolescent speaking with the authority and vocabulary of a powerful adult. Nguyen had heard the name Fowl before – who hadn't in the international underworld? – but he'd assumed he'd be dealing with Artemis Senior, not this boy. Though the word 'boy' hardly seemed to do this gaunt individual justice. And the giant, Butler. It was obvious that he could snap a man's backbone like a twig with those mammoth hands. Nguyen was starting to think that no amount of money was worth another minute in this strange company.

'And now to business,' said Artemis, placing a micro recorder on the table. 'You answered our web advertisement.'

Nguyen nodded, suddenly praying his information was accurate.

'Yes, Mister ... Master Fowl. What you're looking for ... I know where it is.'

'Really? And am I supposed to take your word for this? You could be walking me straight into an ambush. My family is not without enemies.'

Butler snatched a mosquito out of the air beside his employer's ear.

'No, no,' said Nguyen, reaching for his wallet.' 'Here, look.'

Artemis studied the Polaroid. He willed his heart to maintain a calm beat. It seemed promising, but anything could be faked these days with a PC and flatbed scanner. The picture showed a hand reaching from layered shadows. A mottled green hand.

'Hmm,' he murmured. 'Explain.'

'This woman. She is a healer, near Tu Do Street. She works in exchange for rice wine. All the time, drunk.'

Artemis nodded. It made sense. The drinking. One of the few consistent facts his research had unearthed. He stood, smoothing the creases from his white polo shirt.

'Very well. Lead on, Mister Nguyen.'

Nguyen wiped the sweat from his stringy moustache.

'Information only. That was the agreement. I don't want any curses on my head.'

Butler expertly gripped the informant behind the neck.

'I'm sorry, Mister Nguyen, but the time when you had a choice in matters is long past.'

Butler steered the protesting Vietnamese to a rented four-wheel drive that was hardly necessary on the flat streets of Ho Chi Minh City, or Saigon as the locals still called it, but Artemis preferred to be as insulated from civilians as possible.

The jeep inched forward at a painfully slow rate, made all the more excruciating by the anticipation building in Artemis's chest. He could suppress it no longer. Could they at last be at the end of their quest? After six false alarms across three continents, could this wine-sodden healer be the gold at the end of the rainbow? Artemis almost chuckled. Gold at the end of the rainbow. He'd made a joke. Now there's something that didn't happen every day.

The mopeds parted like fish in a giant shoal. There seemed to be no end to the crowds. Even the alleyways were full to bursting with vendors and hagglers. Cooks dropped fish heads into woks of hissing oil, and urchins threaded their way underfoot, searching for unguarded valuables. Others sat in the shade, wearing out their thumbs on Gameboys.

Nguyen was sweating right through his khaki top. It wasn't the humidity, he was used to that. It was this whole cursed situation. He should've known better than to mix magic and crime. He made a silent promise that if he got out of this, he would change his ways. No more answering shady Internet requests, and certainly no more consorting with the sons of European crime lords.

The jeep could go only so far. Eventually the side streets grew too narrow for the four-wheel drive. Artemis turned to Nguyen. 'It seems we must proceed on foot, Mister Nguyen. Run if you like, but expect a sharp and fatal pain between your shoulder blades.'

Nguyen glanced into Butler's eyes. They were a deep blue, almost black. There was no mercy in those eyes. 'Don't worry,' he said. 'I won't run.'

They climbed down from the vehicle. A thousand suspicious eyes followed their progress along the steaming alley. An unfortunate pickpocket attempted to steal Butler's wallet. The manservant broke the man's fingers without looking down. They were given a wide berth after that.

The alley narrowed to a rutted lane. Sewage and drainpipes fed directly on to the muddy surface. Cripples and beggars huddled on rice-mat islands. Most of the residents of this lane had nothing to spare, with the exception of three.

'Well?' demanded Artemis. 'Where is she?'

Nguyen jabbed a finger towards a black triangle beneath a rusted fire escape.

'There. Under there. She never comes out. Even to buy rice spirits, she sends a runner. Now, can I go?'

Artemis didn't bother answering. Instead he picked his way across the puddled lane to the lee of the fire escape. He could discern furtive movements in the shadows.

'Butler, could you hand me the goggles?'

Butler plucked a set of night-vision glasses from his belt and placed them in Artemis's outstretched hand. The focus motor buzzed to suit the light.

Artemis fixed the glasses to his face. Everything became radioactive green. Taking a deep breath, he turned his gaze to the squirming shadows. Something squatted on a raffia mat, shifting uneasily in the almost non-existent light. Artemis fine-tuned the focus. The figure was small, abnormally so, and wrapped in a filthy shawl. Empty spirit jugs were half-buried in the mud around her. One forearm poked from the material. It seemed green. But then, so did everything else.

'Madam,' he said, 'I have a proposition for you.'

The figure's head wobbled sleepily.

'Wine,' she rasped, her voice like nails on a school board. 'Wine, English.'

Artemis smiled. The gift of tongues, aversion to light. Check, check.

'Irish, actually. Now, about my proposition?'

The healer shook a bony finger craftily. 'Wine first. Then talk.'

'Butler?'

The bodyguard reached into a pocket and drew out a half-pint of the finest Irish whiskey. Artemis took the bottle and held it teasingly beyond the shadows. He barely had time to remove his goggles when the claw-like hand darted from the gloom to snatch the whiskey. A mottled green hand. There was no doubt.

Artemis swallowed a triumphant grin.

'Pay our friend, Butler. In full. Remember, Mister Nguyen, this is between us. You don't want Butler to come back, do you?'

'No, no, Master Fowl. My lips are sealed.'

'They had better be. Or Butler will seal them permanently.'

Nguyen skipped off down the alley, so relieved to be alive that he didn't even bother counting the sheaf of US currency. Most unlike him. In any event, it was all there. All twenty thousand dollars. Not bad for half an hour's work.

Artemis turned back to the healer.

'Now, madam, you have something that I want.'

The healer's tongue caught a drop of alcohol at the corner of her mouth.

'Yes, Irish. Sore head. Bad tooth. I heal.'

Artemis replaced the night-vision goggles and squatted to her level.

'I am perfectly healthy, madam, apart from a slight dust-mite allergy, and I don't think even you can do anything about that. No. What I want from you is your Book.'

The hag froze. Bright eyes glinted from beneath the shawl.

'Book?' she said cautiously. 'I don't know about no book. I am healer. You want book, go to library.'

Artemis sighed with exaggerated patience. 'You are no healer. You are a sprite, p'shóg, fairy, ka-dalun. Whichever language you prefer to use. And I want your Book.'

For a long moment the creature said nothing, then she threw back the shawl from her forehead. In the green glow of the night-vision goggles, her features leaped at Artemis like a Hallowe'en mask. The fairy's nose was long and hooked under two slitted golden eyes. Her ears were pointed, and the alcohol addiction had melted her skin like putty.

'If you know about the Book, human,' she said slowly, fighting the numbing effects of the whiskey, 'then you know about the magic I have in my fist. I can kill you with a snap of my fingers!'

Artemis shrugged. 'I think not. Look at you. You are near dead. The rice wine has dulled your senses. Reduced to healing warts. Pathetic. I am here to save you, in return for the Book.'

'What could a human want with our Book?'

'That is no concern of yours. All you need to know are your options.'

The sprite's pointed ears quivered. Options?

'One, you refuse to give us the Book and we go home, leaving you to rot in this sewer.'

'Yes,' said the fairy. 'I choose this option.'

'Ah no. Don't be so eager. If we leave without the Book, you will be dead in a day.'

'A day! A day!' The healer laughed. 'I will outlive you by a century. Even fairies tethered to the human realm can survive the ages.'

'Not with half a pint of holy water inside them,' said Artemis, tapping the now empty whiskey bottle.

The fairy blanched, then screamed, a high keening horrible sound.

'Holy water! You have murdered me, human.'

'True,' admitted Artemis. 'It should start to burn any minute now.'

The fairy poked her stomach tentatively. 'The second option?'

'Listening now, are we? Very well then. Option two. You give me the Book for thirty minutes only. Then I return your magic to you.'

The sprite's jaw dropped. 'Return my magic? Not possible.'

'Oh but it is. I have in my possession two ampoules.

One, a vial of spring water from the fairy well sixty metres below the ring of Tara – possibly the most magical place on earth. This will counteract the holy water.'

'And the other?'

'The other is a little shot of man-made magic. A virus that feeds on alcohol, mixed with a growth reagent. It will flush every drop of rice wine from your body, remove the dependence and even bolster your failing liver. It'll be messy, but after a day you'll be zipping around as though you were a thousand years old again.'

The sprite licked her lips. To be able to rejoin the People? Tempting.

'How do I know to trust you, human? You have tricked me once already.'

'Good point. Here's the deal. I give you the water on faith. Then, after I've had a look at the Book, you get the booster. Take it or leave it.'

The fairy considered. The pain was already curling around her abdomen. She thrust out her wrist.

'I take it.'

'I thought you might. Butler?'

The giant manservant unwrapped a soft Velcroed case containing a syringe gun and two vials. He loaded the clear one, shooting it into the sprite's clammy arm. The fairy stiffened momentarily, and then relaxed.

'Strong magic,' she breathed.

'Yes. But not as strong as your own will be when I give

you the second injection. Now, the Book.'

The sprite reached into the folds of her filthy robe, rummaging for an age. Artemis held his breath. This was it. Soon the Fowls would be great again. A new empire would rise, with Artemis Fowl the Second at its head.

The fairy woman withdrew a closed fist.

'No use to you anyway. Written in the old tongue.'

Artemis nodded, not trusting himself to speak.

She opened her knobbly fingers. Lying in her palm was a tiny golden volume the size of a matchbox.

'Here, human. Thirty of your minutes. No more.'

Butler took the tiny tome reverentially. The bodyguard activated a compact digital camera and began photographing each wafer-thin page of the Book. The process took several minutes. When he was finished, the entire volume was stored on the camera's chip. Artemis preferred not to take chances with information. Airport security equipment had been known to wipe many a vital disk. So he instructed his aide to transfer the file to his portable phone and from there e-mail it to Fowl Manor in Dublin. Before the thirty minutes were up, the file containing every symbol in the Fairy Book was sitting safely in the Fowl server.

Artemis returned the tiny volume to its owner.

'Nice doing business with you.'

The sprite lurched to her knees. 'The other potion, human?'

Artemis smiled. 'Oh yes, the restoring booster. I suppose I did promise.'

'Yes. Human promised.'

'Very well. But before we administer it, I must warn you that purging is not pleasant. You're not going to enjoy this one bit.'

The fairy gestured around her at the squalid filth. 'You think I enjoy this? I want to fly again.'

Butler loaded the second vial, shooting this one straight into the carotid artery.

The sprite immediately collapsed on the mat, her entire frame quivering violently.

'Time to leave,' commented Artemis. 'A hundred years of alcohol leaving a body by any means possible is not a pretty sight.'

The Butlers had been serving the Fowls for centuries. It had always been the way. Indeed there were several eminent linguists of the opinion that this was how the noun originated. The first record of this unusual arrangement was when Virgil Butler had been contracted as servant, bodyguard and cook to Lord Hugo de Fóle for one of the first great Norman crusades.

At the age of ten, Butler children were sent to a private training centre in Israel, where they were taught the specialized skills necessary to guard the latest in the Fowl line. These skills included cordon bleu cooking, marksmanship, a customized blend of martial arts, emergency medicine and information technology. If, at the end of their training, there was not a Fowl to guard, then the Butlers were eagerly snapped up as bodyguards for various royal personages, generally in Monaco or Saudi Arabia.

Once a Fowl and a Butler were put together, they were paired for life. It was a demanding job, and lonely, but the rewards were handsome if you survived to enjoy them. If not, then your family received a six-figure settlement plus a monthly pension.

The current Butler had been guarding young Master Artemis for twelve years, since the moment of his birth. And, though they adhered to the age-old formalities, they were much more than master and servant. Artemis was the closest thing Butler had to a friend, and Butler was the closest Artemis had to a father, albeit one who obeyed orders.

Butler held his tongue until they were aboard the Heathrow connection from Bangkok, then he had to ask.

'Artemis?'

Artemis looked up from the screen of his PowerBook. He was getting a head start on the translation.

'Yes?'

'The sprite. Why didn't we simply keep the Book and leave her to die?'

'A corpse is evidence, Butler. My way, the People will

have no reason to be suspicious.'

'But the sprite?'

'I hardly think she will confess to showing humans the Book. In any case, I mixed a slight amnesiac into her second injection. When she finally wakes up, the last week will be a blur.'

Butler nodded appreciatively. Always two steps ahead, that was Master Artemis. People said he was a chip off the old block. They were wrong. Master Artemis was a brand-new block, the likes of which had never been seen before.

Doubts assuaged, Butler returned to his copy of *Guns and Ammo*, leaving his employer to unravel the secrets of the universe.

CHAPTER 2: TRANSLATION

 BY now, you must have guessed just how far Artemis Fowl was prepared to go in order to achieve his goal. But what exactly was this goal? What outlandish scheme would involve the blackmailing of an alcohol-addicted sprite? The answer was gold.

Artemis's search had begun two years previously when he first became interested in surfing the Internet. He quickly found the more arcane sites: alien abduction, UFO sightings and the supernatural. But most specifically the existence of the People.

Trawling through gigabytes of data, he found hundreds of references to fairies from nearly every country in the world. Each civilization had its own term for the People, but they were undoubtedly members of the same hidden family. Several stories mentioned a Book carried by each fairy. It was their Bible, containing, as it allegedly did, the history of their race and the commandments that governed their extended lives. Of course, this Book was written in Gnommish, the fairy text, and would be of no use to any human.

Artemis believed that with today's technology the Book could be translated. And with this translation you could begin to exploit a whole new group of creatures.

Know thine enemy was Artemis's motto, so he immersed himself in the lore of the People until he had compiled a huge database on their characteristics. But it wasn't enough. So Artemis put out a call on the Web: Irish businessman will pay large amount of US dollars to meet a fairy, sprite, leprechaun, pixie. The responses had been mostly fraudulent, but Ho Chi Minh City had paid off.

Artemis was perhaps the only person alive who could take full advantage of his recent acquisition. He still retained a childlike belief in magic, tempered by an adult determination to exploit it. If there was anybody capable of relieving the fairies of some of their magical gold, it was Artemis Fowl the Second.

It was early morning before they reached Fowl Manor. Artemis was anxious to bring up the file on his computer, but first he decided to call in on Mother.

Angeline Fowl was bedridden. She had been since her husband's disappearance. Nervous tension, the physicians said. Nothing for it but rest and sleeping pills. That was almost a year ago.

Butler's little sister, Juliet, was sitting at the foot of the stairs. Her gaze was boring a hole in the wall. Even the glitter mascara couldn't soften her expression. Artemis had seen that look already, just before Juliet had suplexed a particularly cheeky pizza boy. The suplex, Artemis gathered, was a wrestling move. An unusual obsession for a teenage girl. But then again she was, after all, a Butler.

'Problems, Juliet?'

Juliet straightened hurriedly. 'My own fault, Artemis. Apparently I left a gap in the curtains. Mrs Fowl couldn't sleep.'

'Hmm,' muttered Artemis, scaling the oak staircase slowly.

He worried about his mother's condition. She hadn't seen the light of day in a long time now. Then again, should she miraculously recover, emerging revitalized from her bedchamber, it would signal the end of Artemis's own extraordinary freedom. It would be back off to school, and no more spearheading criminal enterprises for you, my lad.

He knocked gently on the arched double doors.

'Mother? Are you awake?'

Something smashed against the other side of the door. It sounded expensive.

'Of course I'm awake! How can I sleep in this blinding glare?'

Artemis ventured inside. An antique four-poster bed

threw shadowy spires in the darkness, and a pale sliver of light poked through a gap in the velvet curtains. Angeline Fowl sat hunched on the bed, her pale limbs glowing white in the gloom.

'Artemis, darling, where have you been?'

Artemis sighed. She recognized him. That was a good sign.

'School trip, Mother. Skiing in Austria.'

'Ah, skiing,' crooned Angeline. 'How I miss it. Maybe when your father returns.'

Artemis felt a lump in his throat. Most uncharacteristic.

'Yes. Perhaps when Father returns.'

'Darling, could you close those wretched curtains. The light is intolerable.'

'Of course, Mother.'

Artemis felt his way across the room, wary of the low-level clothes chests scattered about the floor. Finally his fingers curled around the velvet drapes. For a moment he was tempted to throw them wide open, then he sighed and closed the gap.

'Thank you, darling. By the way, we really have to get rid of that maid. She is good for absolutely nothing.'

Artemis held his tongue. Juliet had been a hard-working and loyal member of the Fowl household for the past three years. Time to use Mother's absent-mindedness to his advantage.

'You're right of course, Mother. I've been meaning to

do it for some time. Butler has a sister I believe would be perfect for the position. I think I've mentioned her. Juliet?'

Angeline frowned. 'Juliet? Yes, the name does seem familiar. Well, anyone would be better than that silly girl we have now. When can she start?'

'Straight away. I'll have Butler fetch her from the lodge.'

'You're a good boy, Artemis. Now give Mummy a hug.'

Artemis stepped into the shadowy folds of his mother's robe. She smelled perfumed, like petals in water. But her arms were cold and weak.

'Oh, darling,' she whispered, and the sound sent goosebumps popping down Artemis's neck. 'I hear things. At night. They crawl along the pillows and into my ears.'

Artemis felt that lump in his throat again.

'Perhaps we should open the curtains, Mother.'

'No,' his mother sobbed, releasing him from her grasp. 'No. Because then I could see them too.'

'Mother, please.'

But it was no use. Angeline was gone. She crawled to the far corner of the bed, pulling the quilt under her chin.

'Send the new girl.'

'Yes, Mother.'

'Send her with cucumber slices and water.'

'Yes, Mother.'

Angeline glared at him with crafty eyes. 'And stop calling me Mother. I don't know who you are, but you're certainly not my little Arty.'

Artemis blinked back a few rebellious tears. 'Of course. Sorry, Moth – Sorry.'

'Hmm. Don't come back here again, or I'll have my husband take care of you. He's a very important man, you know.'

'Very well, Mrs Fowl. This is the last you'll see of me.'

'It had better be.' Angeline froze suddenly. 'Do you hear them?'

Artemis shook his head. 'No. I don't hear any –'

'They're coming for me. They're everywhere.'

Angeline dived for cover beneath the bedclothes. Artemis could still hear her terrified sobs as he descended the marble staircase.

The Book was proving far more stubborn than Artemis had anticipated. It seemed to be almost actively resisting him. No matter which program he ran it through, the computer came up blank.

Artemis hard-copied every page, tacking them to the walls of his study. Sometimes it helped to have things on paper. The script was like nothing he'd seen before, and yet it was strangely familiar. Obviously a mixture of symbolic and character-based language, the text meandered around the page in no apparent order.

What the program needed was some frame of reference, some central point on which to build. He separated all the characters and ran comparisons with English, Chinese, Greek, Arabic and Cyrillic texts, even with Ogham. Nothing.

Moody with frustration, Artemis sent Juliet scurrying when she interrupted with sandwiches, and moved on to symbols. The most frequently recurring pictogram was a small male figure. Male, he presumed, though with the limited knowledge of the fairy anatomy he supposed it could be female. A thought struck him. Artemis opened the ancient languages file on his Power Translator and selected Egyptian.

At last. A hit. The male symbol was remarkably similar to the Anubis god representation on Tutankhamen's inner-chamber hieroglyphics. This was consistent with his other findings. The first written human stories were about fairies, suggesting that their civilization predated man's own. It would seem that the Egyptians had simply adapted an existing scripture to suit their needs.

There were other resemblances. But the characters were just dissimilar enough to slip through the computer's net. This would have to be done manually. Each Gnommish figure had to be enlarged, printed and then compared with the hieroglyphs.

Artemis felt the excitement of success thumping inside his ribcage. Almost every fairy pictogram or letter had an Egyptian counterpart. Most were universal, such as the sun or birds. But some seemed exclusively supernatural

and had to be tailored to fit. The Anubis figure, for
example, would make no sense as a dog god, so Artemis
altered it to read king of the fairies.

By midnight, Artemis had successfully fed his findings
into the Macintosh. All he had to do now was press
'Decode'. He did so. What emerged was a long, intricate
string of meaningless gibberish.

A normal child would have abandoned the task long
since. The average adult would probably have been
reduced to slapping the keyboard. But not Artemis. This
book was testing him and he would not allow it to win.

The letters were right, he was certain of it. It was just
the order that was wrong. Rubbing the sleep from his
eyes, Artemis glared at the pages again. Each segment was
bordered by a solid line. This could represent paragraphs
or chapters, but they were not meant to be read in the
usual left to right, top to bottom fashion.

Artemis experimented. He tried the Arabic right to
left and the Chinese columns. Nothing worked. Then he
noticed that each page had one thing in common – a
central section. The other pictograms were arranged
around this pivotal area. So a central starting point
perhaps. But where to go from there? Artemis scanned
the pages for some other common factor. After several
minutes he found it. There was on each page a tiny
spearhead in the corner of one section. Could this be an
arrow? A direction? Go this way? So the theory would be

start in the middle, then follow the arrow, reading in spirals.

The computer program wasn't built to handle something like this, so Artemis had to improvise. With a craft knife and ruler, he dissected the first page of the Book and reassembled it in the traditional Western languages order – left to right, parallel rows. Then he rescanned the page and fed it through the modified Egyptian translator.

The computer hummed and whirred, converting all the information to binary. Several times it stopped to ask for confirmation of a character or symbol. This happened less and less as the machine learned the new language. Eventually two words flashed on the screen: **File converted.**

Fingers shaking from exhaustion and excitement, Artemis clicked 'Print'. A single page scrolled from the LaserWriter. It was in English now. Yes, there were mistakes, some fine-tuning needed, but it was perfectly legible and, more importantly, perfectly understandable.

Fully aware that he was probably the first human in several thousand years to decode the magical words, Artemis switched on his desk light and began to read.

The Booke of the People.
Being instructions to our magicks and life rules

Carry me always, carry me well.
I am thy teacher of herb and spell.
I am thy link to power arcane.
Forget me and thy magick shall wane.

Ten times ten commandments there be.
They will answer every mystery.

Cures, curses, alchemy.
These secrets shall be thine, through me.

But, Fairy, remember this above all.
I am not for those in mud that crawl.
And forever doomed shall be the one,
Who betrays my secrets one by one.

Artemis could hear the blood pumping in his ears. He had them. They would be as ants beneath his feet. Their every secret would be laid bare by technology. Suddenly the exhaustion claimed him and he sank back in his chair. There was so much yet to complete. Forty-three pages to be translated for a start.

He pressed the intercom button that linked him to speakers all over the house. 'Butler. Get Juliet and come up here. There are some jigsaws I need you to assemble.'

Perhaps a little family history would be useful at this point.

The Fowls were, indeed, legendary criminals. For generations they had skirmished on the wrong side of the law, hoarding enough funds to become legitimate. Of course, once they were legitimate they found it not to their liking and returned almost immediately to crime.

It was Artemis the First, our subject's father, who had thrown the family fortune into jeopardy. With the break-up of communist Russia, Artemis Senior had decided to invest a huge chunk of the Fowl fortune in establishing new shipping lines to the vast continent. New consumers, he reasoned, would need new consumer goods. The Russian Mafia did not take too kindly to a Westerner muscling in on their market and so decided to send a little message. This message took the form of a stolen Stinger missile launched at the *Fowl Star* on her way past Murmansk. Artemis Senior was on board the ship, along with Butler's uncle and 250,000 cans of cola. It was quite an explosion.

The Fowls were not left destitute, far from it. But billionaire status was no longer theirs. Artemis the Second vowed to remedy this. He would restore the family fortune. And he would do it in his own unique fashion.

Once the Book was translated, Artemis could begin planning in earnest. He already knew what the ultimate goal was, now he could figure out how to achieve it.

Gold, of course, was the objective. The acquisition of gold. It seemed that the People were almost as fond of the precious metal as humans. Each fairy had its own cache, but not for much longer if Artemis had his way. There would be at least one of the fairy folk wandering around with empty pockets by the time he'd finished.

After eighteen solid hours of sleep and a light continental breakfast, Artemis climbed to the study that he had inherited from his father. It was a traditional enough room — dark oak and floor-to-ceiling shelving — but Artemis had jammed it with the latest computer technology. A series of networked AppleMacs whirred from various corners of the room. One was running CNN's web site through a DAT projector, throwing oversized current-affairs images against the back wall.

Butler was there already, firing up the hard drives.

'Shut them all down, except the Book. I need quiet for this.'

The manservant started. The CNN site had been running for almost a year. Artemis was convinced that news of his father's rescue would come from there. Shutting it down meant that he was finally letting go.

'All of them?'

Artemis glanced at the back wall for a moment. 'Yes,' he said finally. 'All of them.'

Butler took the liberty of patting his employer gently on the shoulder, just once, before returning to work. Artemis cracked his knuckles. Time to do what he did best — plot dastardly acts.

CHAPTER 3: **HOLLY**

HOLLY Short was lying in bed having a silent fume. Nothing unusual about this. Leprechauns in general were not known for their geniality. But Holly was in an exceptionally bad mood, even for a fairy. Technically she was an elf, fairy being a general term. She was a leprechaun too, but that was just a job.

Perhaps a description would be more helpful than a lecture on fairy genealogy. Holly Short had nut-brown skin, cropped auburn hair and hazel eyes. Her nose had a hook and her mouth was plump and cherubic, which was appropriate considering that Cupid was her great-grandfather. Her mother was a European elf with a fiery temper and a willowy figure. Holly, too, had a slim frame, with long tapered fingers perfect for wrapping around a buzz baton. Her ears, of course, were pointed. At exactly one metre in height, Holly was only a centimetre below the fairy average, but even one centimetre can make an awful lot of difference when you don't have many to spare.

Commander Root was the cause of Holly's distress. Root had been on Holly's case since day one. The commander had decided to take offence at the fact that the first female officer in Recon's history had been assigned to his squad. Recon was a notoriously dangerous posting with a high fatality rate, and Root didn't think it was any place for a girlie. Well, he was just going to have to get used to the idea, because Holly Short had no intention of quitting for him or anybody else.

Though she'd never admit it, another possible cause for Holly's irritability was the Ritual. She'd been meaning to perform it for several moons now, but somehow there just never seemed to be time. And if Root found out she was running low on magic, she'd be transferred to Traffic for sure.

Holly rolled off her futon and stumbled into the shower. That was one advantage of living near the earth's core – the water was always hot. No natural light, of course, but that was a small price to pay for privacy. Underground. The last human-free zone. There was nothing like coming home after a long day on the job, switching off your shield and sinking into a bubbling slime pool. Bliss.

The fairy suited up, zipping the dull-green jumpsuit up to her chin and strapping on her helmet. LEPrecon uniforms were smart these days. Not like that top-o'-the-morning costume the force had had to wear back in the old days. Buckled shoes and knickerbockers! Honestly. No wonder leprechauns were such ridiculous figures in human folklore. Still, probably better that way. If the Mud People knew that the word 'leprechaun' actually originated from LEPrecon, an elite branch of the Lower Elements Police, they'd probably take steps to stamp them out. Better to stay inconspicuous and let the humans have their stereotypes.

With the moon already rising on the surface, there was no time for a proper breakfast. Holly grabbed the remains of a nettle smoothie from the cooler and drank it in the tunnels. As usual there was chaos in the main thoroughfare. Airborne sprites jammed the avenue like stones in a bottle. The gnomes weren't helping either, lumbering along with their big swinging behinds blocking two lanes. Swear toads infested every damp patch, cursing like sailors. That particular breed began as a joke but had multiplied into an epidemic. Someone lost their wand over that one.

Holly battled through the crowds to the police station. There was already a riot outside Spud's Spud Emporium. LEP Corporal Newt was trying to sort it out. Good luck to him. Nightmare. At least Holly got the chance to work above ground.

The LEP station doors were crammed with protesters.

The goblin/dwarf turf war had flared up again, and every morning hordes of angry parents showed up demanding the release of their innocent offspring. Holly snorted. If there actually was an innocent goblin, Holly Short had yet to meet him. They were clogging up the cells now, howling gang chants and hurling fireballs at each other.

Holly shouldered her way into the throng. 'Coming through,' she grunted. 'Police business.'

They were on her like flies on a stink-worm.

'My Grumpo is innocent!'

'Police brutality!'

'Officer, could you take my baby in his blanky? He can't sleep without it.'

Holly set her visor to reflect and ignored them all. Once upon a time the uniform would have earned you some respect. Not any more. Now you were a target. 'Excuse me, Officer, but I seem to have misplaced my jar of warts.' 'Pardon me, young elf, but my cat's climbed a stalactite.' Or, 'If you have a minute, Captain, could you tell me how to get to the Fountain of Youth?' Holly shuddered. Tourists. She had troubles of her own. More than she knew, as she was about to find out.

In the station lobby, a kleptomaniac dwarf was busy picking the pockets of everyone else in the booking line, including the officer he was handcuffed to. Holly gave him a swipe in the backside with her buzz baton. The electric charge singed the seat of his leather trousers.

'Whatcha doing there, Mulch?'

Mulch started, contraband dropping from his sleeves.

'Officer Short,' he whined, his face a mask of regret, 'I can't help myself. It's my nature.'

'I know that, Mulch. And it's our nature to throw you in a cell for a couple of centuries.'

She winked at the dwarf's arresting officer.

'Nice to see you're staying alert.'

The elf blushed, kneeling to pick up his wallet and badge.

Holly forged past Root's office, hoping she would make it to her cubicle before …

'SHORT! GET IN HERE!'

Holly sighed. Ah well. Here we go again.

Stowing her helmet under her arm, Holly smoothed the creases from her uniform and stepped into Commander Root's office.

Root's face was purple with rage. This was more or less his general state of existence, a fact that had earned him the nickname 'Beetroot'. There was an office pool running on how long he had before his heart exploded. The smart money was on half a century, at the outside.

Commander Root was tapping the moonometer on his wrist. 'Well?' he demanded. 'What time do you call this?'

Holly could feel her own face colouring. She was barely a minute late. There were at least a dozen officers on this shift who hadn't even reported in yet. But Root always singled her out for persecution.

'The thoroughfare,' she mumbled lamely. 'There were four lanes down.'

'Don't insult me with your excuses!' roared the commander. 'You know what the city centre is like! Get up a few minutes earlier!'

It was true, she did know what Haven was like. Holly Short was a city elf born and bred. Since the humans began experimenting with mineral drilling, more and more fairies had been driven out of the shallow forts and into the depth and security of Haven City. The metropolis was overcrowded and under-serviced. And now there was a lobby to allow automobiles in the pedestrianized city centre. As if the place wasn't smelly enough already with all those country gnomes lumbering around the place.

Root was right. She should get up a bit earlier. But she wouldn't. Not until everybody else was forced to.

'I know what you're thinking,' said Root. 'Why am I picking on you every day? Why don't I ever bawl out those other layabouts?'

Holly said nothing, but agreement was written all over her face.

'I'll tell you why, shall I?'

Holly risked a nod.

'It's because you're a girl.'

Holly felt her fingers curl into fists. She knew it!

'But not for the reasons you think,' continued Root.

'You are the first girl in Recon. Ever. You are a test case. A beacon. There are a million fairies out there watching your every move. There are a lot of hopes riding on you. But there is a lot of prejudice against you too. The future of law enforcement is in your hands. And at the moment, I'd say it was a little heavy.'

Holly blinked. Root had never said anything like this before. Usually it was just 'Fix your helmet', 'Stand up straight', blah blah blah.

'You have to be the best you can be, Short, and that has to be better than anybody else.' Root sighed, sinking into his swivel chair. 'I don't know, Holly. Ever since that Hamburg affair.'

Holly winced. The Hamburg affair had been a total disaster. One of her perps had skipped out to the surface and tried to bargain with the Mud People for asylum. Root had to stop time, call in the Retrieval Squad, and do four memory wipes. A lot of police time wasted. All her fault.

The commander took a form from his desk. 'It's no use. I've made up my mind. I'm putting you on Traffic and bringing in Corporal Frond.'

'Frond!' exploded Holly. 'She's a bimbo. An airhead. You can't make her the test case!'

Root's face turned an even deeper shade of purple.

'I can and I will. Why shouldn't I? You have never given me your best ... Either that or your best just isn't good enough. Sorry, Short, you had your chance ...'

The commander turned back to his paperwork. The meeting was over. Holly could only stand there, aghast. She'd blown it. The best career opportunity she was ever likely to get and she'd tossed it in the gutter. One mistake and her future was past. It wasn't fair. Holly felt an uncharacteristic anger take hold of her, but she swallowed it. This was no time to lose her temper.

'Commander Root, sir. I feel I deserve one more chance.'

Root didn't even look up from the paperwork. 'And why's that?'

Holly took a deep breath. 'Because of my record, sir. It speaks for itself, apart from the Hamburg thing. Ten successful recons. Not a single memory wipe or time-stop, apart from ...'

'The Hamburg thing,' completed Root.

Holly took a chance. 'If I were a male — one of your precious sprites — we wouldn't even be having this conversation.'

Root glanced up sharply. 'Now, just a minute, Captain Short —'

He was interrupted by the bleeping of one of the phones on his desk. Then two, then three. A giant viewscreen crackled into life on the wall behind him.

Root jabbed the speaker button, putting all the callers on conference.

◊ ⌂ ⟩ ᛒ ⚘ · ⚭ ⚼ · ⊕ ▢ · ⟩ ⚘ · ⫙ ᛒ →

'Yes?'

'We've got a runner.'

Root nodded. 'Anything on Scopes?'

Scopes was the shop name for the shrouded trackers attached to American communications satellites.

'Yep,' said caller two. 'Big blip in Europe. Southern Italy. No shield.'

Root cursed. An unshielded fairy could be seen by mortal eyes. That wasn't so bad if the perp was humanoid.

'Classification?'

'Bad news, Commander,' said the third caller. 'We got us a rogue troll.'

Root rubbed his eyes. Why did these things always happen on his watch? Holly could understand his frustration. Trolls were the meanest of the deep-tunnel creatures. They wandered the labyrinth, preying on anything unlucky enough to cross their path. Their tiny brains had no room for rules or restraint. Occasionally one found its way into the shaft of a pressure elevator. Usually the concentrated air current fried them, but sometimes one survived and was blasted to the surface. Driven crazy by pain and even the tiniest amount of light, they would generally proceed to destroy everything in their path.

Root shook his head rapidly, recovering himself.

'OK, Captain Short. Looks like you get your chance. You're running hot, I take it?'

'Yes, sir,' lied Holly, all too aware that Root would suspend her immediately if he knew she'd neglected the Ritual.

'Good. Then sign yourself out a side-arm and proceed to the target area.'

Holly glanced at the viewscreen. Scopes were sending high-res shots of an Italian fortified town. A red dot was moving rapidly through the countryside towards the human population.

'Do a thorough reconnaissance and report in. Do not attempt a retrieval. Is that understood?'

'Yessir.'

'We lost six men to troll attacks last quarter. Six men. That was below ground, in familiar territory.'

'I understand, sir.'

Root pursed his lips doubtfully.

'Do you understand, Short? Do you really?'

'I think so, sir.'

'Have you ever seen what a troll can do to flesh and bone?'

'No, sir. Not up close.'

'Good. Let's not make today your first time.'

'Understood.'

Root glared at her. 'I don't know why it is, Captain Short, but whenever you start agreeing with me, I get decidedly nervous.'

Root was right to be nervous. If he'd known how this

straightforward Recon assignment was going to turn out, he would probably have retired there and then. Tonight, history was going to be made. And it wasn't the discovery-of-radium, first-man-on-the-moon happy kind of history. It was the Spanish-Inquisition, here-comes-the-Hindenburg bad kind of history. Bad for humans and fairies. Bad for everyone.

Holly proceeded directly to the chutes. Her normally chatty mouth was a grim slash of determination. One chance, that was it. She would allow nothing to break her concentration.

There was the usual queue of holiday visa hopefuls stretching to the corner of Elevator Plaza, but Holly bypassed it by waving her badge at the waiting line. A truculent gnome refused to yield.

'How come you LEP guys get to go topside? What's so special about you?'

Holly breathed deeply through her nose. Courtesy at all times. 'Police business, sir. Now if you could just excuse me.'

The gnome scratched his massive behind. 'I hear you LEP guys make up your police business just to get a look at some moonlight. That's what I hear.'

Holly attempted an amused smile. What actually formed on her lips resembled a lemon-sucking grimace.

'Whoever told you that is an idiot ... sir. Recon

venture only above ground when absolutely necessary.'

The gnome frowned. Obviously he had made up the rumour himself and suspected that Holly might have just called him an idiot. By the time he'd figured it out, she had skipped through the double doors.

Foaly was waiting for her in Ops. Foaly was a paranoid centaur, convinced that human intelligence agencies were monitoring his transport and surveillance network. To prevent them reading his mind, he wore a tinfoil hat at all times.

He glanced up sharply when Holly entered through the pneumatic double doors.

'Anybody see you come in here?'

Holly thought about it.

'The FBI, CIA, NSA, DEA, MI6. Oh and the EIB.'

Foaly frowned. 'The EIB?'

'Everyone in the building,' smirked Holly.

Foaly rose from his swivel chair and clip-clopped over to her.

'Oh, you're very funny, Short. A regular riot. I thought the Hamburg affair might have knocked some of the cockiness out of you. If I were you, I'd concentrate on the job in hand.'

Holly composed herself. He was right.

'OK, Foaly. Fill me in.'

The centaur pointed to a live feed from the Eurosat, which was displayed on a large plasma screen.

'This red dot is the troll. He's moving towards Martina Franca, a fortified town near the city of Brindisi. As far as we can tell, he stumbled into vent E7. It was on cooldown after a surface shot, that's why the troll isn't crispy barbecue right now.'

Holly grimaced. Charming, she thought.

'We've been lucky in that our target has bumped into some food along the way. He chewed on a couple of cows for an hour or two, so that bought us a bit of time.'

'A couple of cows?' exclaimed Holly. 'Just how big is this fellow?'

Foaly adjusted his foil bonnet. 'Bull troll. Fully grown. One hundred and eighty kilos, with tusks like a wild boar. A really wild boar.'

Holly swallowed. Suddenly Recon seemed a much better job than Retrieval.

'Right. What have you got for me?'

Foaly cantered across to the equipment table. He selected what looked like a rectangular wristwatch.

'Locator. You find him, we find you. Routine stuff.'

'Video?'

The centaur clipped a small cylinder into the accommodating groove on Holly's helmet.

'Live feed. Nuclear battery. No time limit. The mike is voice-activated.'

'Good,' said Holly. 'Root said I should take a weapon on this one. Just in case.'

'Way ahead of you,' said Foaly. He picked a platinum handgun from the pile. 'A Neutrino 2000. The latest model. Even the tunnel gangs don't have these. Three settings, if you don't mind. Scorched, well done and crisped to a cinder. Nuclear power source too, so plug away. This baby will outlive you by a thousand years.'

Holly strapped the lightweight weapon into her shoulder holster.

'I'm ready ... I think.'

Foaly chuckled. 'I doubt it. No one's ever really ready for a troll.'

'Thanks for the confidence booster.'

'Confidence is ignorance,' advised the centaur. 'If you're feeling cocky, it's because there's something you don't know.'

Holly thought about arguing, but didn't. Maybe it was because she had a sneaking suspicion that Foaly was right.

The pressure elevators were powered by gaseous columns vented from the earth's core. The LEP tech boys, under Foaly's guidance, had fashioned titanium eggs that could ride on the currents. They had their own independent motors, but for an express ride to the surface there was nothing like the blast from a tidal flare.

Foaly led her past a long line of chute bays to E7. The pod sat in its clamp, looking very fragile to be rocketing about on magma streams. Its underside was charred black and pockmarked from shrapnel.

The centaur slapped it fondly on a fender. 'This baby's been in service for fifty years. Oldest model still in the chutes.'

Holly swallowed. The chutes made her nervous enough without riding in an antique.

'When does it come off-line?'

Foaly scratched his hairy belly. 'With funding the way it is, not until we have us a fatality.'

Holly cranked open the heavy door, the rubber seal yielding with a hiss. The pod was not built for comfort. There was barely enough space for a restraining seat among the jumble of electronics.

'What's that?' asked Holly, pointing at a greyish stain on the seat's headrest.

Foaly shuffled uncomfortably.

'Erm … brain fluid, I think. We had a pressure leak on the last mission. But that's plugged now. And the officer lived. Down a few IQ points, but alive, and he can still take liquids.'

'Well, that's all right then,' quipped Holly, threading her way through the mass of wires.

Foaly strapped the harness on to her, checking the restraints thoroughly.

'All set?'

Holly nodded.

Foaly tapped her helmet mike. 'Keep in touch,' he said, pulling the door behind him.

Don't think about it, Holly told herself. Don't think about the white-hot magma flow that's going to engulf this tiny craft. Don't think about hurtling towards the surface with a MACH 2 force trying to turn you inside-out. And certainly don't think about the blood-crazed troll ready to disembowel you with his tusks. Nope. Don't think about any of that stuff … Too late.

Foaly's voice sounded in her earpiece. 'T-minus twenty,' he said. 'We're on a secure channel in case the Mud People have started underground monitoring. You never know. An oil tanker from the Middle East intercepted a transmission one time. What a mess that was.'

Holly adjusted her helmet mike.

'Focus, Foaly. My life is in your hands here.'

'Uh … OK, sorry. We're going to use the rail to drop you into E7's main shaft, there's a surge due any minute. That should see you past the first hundred klicks, then you're on your own.'

Holly nodded, curling her fingers around the twin joysticks.

'All systems check. Fire it up.'

There was a whoosh as the pod's engines ignited. The tiny craft jostled in its housing, shaking Holly like a bead in a rattle. She could barely hear Foaly speaking into her ear.

'You're in the secondary shaft now. Get ready to fly, Short.'

Holly pulled a rubber cylinder from the dash and slipped it between her teeth. No good having a radio if you've swallowed your tongue. She activated the external cameras and put the view on screen.

The entrance to E7 was creeping towards her. The air was shimmering in the landing-light glow. White-hot sparks tumbled into the secondary shaft. Holly couldn't hear the roar, but she could imagine it. A raw skinning wind like a million trolls howling.

Her fingers tightened around the joysticks. The pod shuddered to a halt at the lip. The chute stretched above and below. Massive. Boundless. Like dropping an ant down a drainpipe.

'Right-o,' crackled Foaly. 'Hold on to your breakfast. Rollercoasters ain't got nothing on this.'

Holly nodded. She couldn't speak, not with the rubber in her mouth. The centaur would be able to see her in the podcam anyway.

'*Sayonara*, sweetheart,' said Foaly, and pressed the button.

The pod's clamp tilted, rolling Holly into the abyss. Her stomach tightened as G-force took hold, dragging her to the centre of the earth. The seismology section had a million probes down here, with a 99.8 success rate at predicting the magma flares. But there was always that point two per cent.

The fall seemed to last for an eternity. And just when Holly had mentally consigned herself to the scrap heap, she felt it. That unforgettable vibration. The feeling that, outside her tiny sphere, the whole world was being shaken apart. Here it comes.

'Fins,' she said, spitting the word around the cylinder.

Foaly may have replied, she couldn't hear him any more. Holly couldn't even hear herself, but she did see the stabilization fins slide out on the monitor.

The flare caught her like a hurricane, spinning the pod at first until the fins caught. Half-melted rocks pelted the craft's underside, jolting it towards the chute walls. Holly compensated with bursts from the joysticks.

The heat was tremendous in the confined space, enough to fry a human. But fairy lungs are made of stronger stuff. The acceleration dragged at her body with invisible hands, stretching the flesh over her arms and face. Holly blinked salty sweat from her eyes and concentrated on the monitor. The flare had totally engulfed her pod, and it was a big one too. Force seven at the very least. A good 500-metre girth. Orange-striped magma swirled and hissed around her, searching for a weak point in the metal casing.

The pod groaned and complained, fifty-year-old rivets threatening to pop. Holly shook her head. The first thing she was going to do on her return was kick Foaly straight in the hairy behind. She felt like a nut inside a shell, between a gnome's molars. Doomed.

A bow plate buckled, popped in as though punched by a giant fist. The pressure light blinked on. Holly could feel her head being squeezed. The eyes would be first to go — popping like ripe berries.

She checked the dials. Twenty more seconds before she rode out the flare and was running on thermals. Those twenty seconds seemed like an age. Holly sealed the helmet to protect her eyes, riding out the final barrage of rocks.

And suddenly they were clear, sailing upwards on the comparatively gentle spirals of hot air. Holly added her own thrusters to the upward force. No time to waste floating around on the wind.

Above her, a circle of neon lights marked the docking zone. Holly swivelled horizontal and pointed the docking nodes at the lights. This was delicate. Many Recon pilots had made it this far, only to miss the port and lose valuable time. Not Holly. She was a natural. First in the academy.

She gave the thrusters one final squeeze and coasted the last hundred metres. Using the rudders beneath her feet, she teased the pod through the circle of light and into its clamp on the landing pad. The nodes revolved, settling into their grooves. Safe.

Holly smacked herself on the chest, releasing the safety harness. Once the door seal was open, sweet surface air flooded the cabin. There was nothing like that first breath after a ride in the chutes. She breathed deeply, purging the stale pod air from her lungs. How had the People ever left the surface? Sometimes she wished that her ancestors had stayed to fight it out with the Mud People, but there were too many of them. Unlike fairies, who could produce only a single child every twenty years, Mud People bred like rodents. Numbers would subdue even magic.

Although she was enjoying the night air, Holly could taste traces of pollutants. The Mud People destroyed everything they came into contact with. Of course they didn't live in the mud any more. Not in this country, at least. Oh no. Big fancy dwellings with rooms for everything – rooms for sleeping, rooms for eating, even a room to go to the toilet! Indoors! Holly shuddered. Imagine going to the toilet inside your own house. Disgusting! The only good thing about going to the toilet was the minerals being returned to the earth, but the Mud People had even managed to botch that up by treating the ... stuff ... with bottles of blue chemicals. If anyone had told her a hundred years ago that humans would be taking the fertile out of fertilizer, she would have told them to get some air holes drilled in their skull.

Holly unhooked a set of wings from their bracket. They were double ovals, with a clunky motor. She moaned. Dragonflies. She hated that model. Petrol engine, if you don't mind. And heavier than a pig dipped in mud. Now the Hummingbird Z7, that was transport. Whisper silent, with a satellite-bounced solar battery that would fly you twice around the world. But there were budget cuts again.

On her wrist, the locator began to beep. She was in range. Holly stepped out of the pod and on to the landing bay. She was inside a camouflaged mound of earth, commonly known as a fairy fort. Indeed, the People used to live in these until they were driven deeper underground. There wasn't much technology. Just a few external monitors, and a self-destruct device should the bay be discovered.

There was nothing on the screens. All clear. The pneumatic doors were slightly askew where the troll had barged through, but otherwise everything seemed operational. Holly strapped on the wings, stepping into the outside world.

The Italian night sky was crisp and brisk, infused with olives and vine. Crickets clicked in the rough grass and moths fluttered in the starlight. Holly couldn't stop herself smiling. It was worth the risk, every bit of it.

Speaking of risk ... She checked the locator. The bip was much stronger now. The troll was almost at the town walls! She could appreciate nature after the mission was over. Now it was time for action.

Holly primed the wings' motor, pulling the starter cord over her shoulder. Nothing. She fumed silently.

Every spoilt kid in Haven had a Hummingbird for their wilderness holidays, and here were the LEP with wings that were junk when they were new. She yanked the cord again and then again. On the third wrench it caught, spewing a stream of smoke and fumes into the night. 'About time,' she grunted, flicking the throttle wide open. The wings flapped their way up to a steady beat and, with not a little effort, lifted Captain Holly Short into the night sky.

Even without the locator, the troll would have been easy to follow. It had left a trail of destruction wider than a tunnel excavator. Holly flew low, skipping between mist hazes and trees, matching the troll's course. The crazed creature had cut a swathe through the middle of a vineyard, turned a stone wall to rubble and left a guard dog gibbering under a hedge. Then she flew over the cows. It was not a pretty sight. Without going into details, let's just say that there wasn't much left besides horns and hooves.

The red bip was louder now. Louder meant closer. She could see the town below her, nestled on top of a low hill, surrounded by a crenellated wall from the Middle Ages. Lights still burned in most windows. Time for a little magic.

A lot of the magic attributed to the People is just superstition. But they do have certain powers. Healing, the *mesmer* and shielding being among them. Shielding is really a misnomer. What fairies actually do is to vibrate at such a high frequency that they are never in one place long enough to be seen. Humans may notice a slight shimmer in the air if they are paying close attention – which they rarely are. And even then the shimmer is generally attributed to evaporation. Typical of Mud People to invent a complicated explanation for a simple phenomenon.

Holly switched on her shield. It took a bit more out of her than usual. She could feel the strain in the beads of sweat on her forehead. I really *should* complete the Ritual, she thought. The sooner the better.

Some commotion below broke into her thoughts. Something that didn't gel with the night-time noises. Holly adjusted the trim on her backpack and flew in for a closer look. Look only, she reminded herself, that was her job. A Recon officer was sent up the chutes to pinpoint the target, while the Retrieval boys took a nice cushy shuttle.

The troll was directly below her, pounding against the town's outer wall, which was coming away in chunks beneath his powerful fingers. Holly sucked in a startled gasp. This guy was a monster! Big as an elephant and ten times as mean. But this particular beast was worse than mean, he was scared.

'Control,' said Holly into her mike. 'Runner located. Situation critical topside.'

Root himself was on the other end of the comlink.

'Clarify, Captain.'

Holly pointed her video link at the troll.

'Runner is going through the town wall. Contact imminent. How far away are Retrieval?'

'ETA five minutes minimum. We're still in the shuttle.'

Holly bit her lip. Root was in the shuttle?

'That's too long, Commander. This whole town is going to explode in ten seconds ... I'm going in.'

'Negative, Holly ... Captain Short. You don't have an invite. You know the law. Hold your position.'

'But, Commander —'

Root cut her off. 'No! No buts, Captain. Hang back. That's an order!'

Holly's entire body felt like a heartbeat. Petrol fumes were addling her brain. What could she do? What was the right decision to make? Lives or orders?

Then the troll broke through the wall and a child's voice split the night.

'*Aiuto!*' it screamed.

Help. An invitation. At a stretch.

'Sorry, Commander. The troll is light-crazy and there are children in there.'

She could imagine Root's face, purple with rage as he spat into the mike.

'I'll have your stripes, Short! You'll spend the next hundred years on drain duty!'

But it was no use. Holly had disconnected her mike and swooped in after the troll.

Streamlining her body, Captain Short ducked into the hole. She appeared to be in a restaurant. A packed restaurant. The troll had been temporarily blinded by the electric light and was thrashing about in the centre of the floor.

The patrons were stunned. Even the child's plea had petered out. They sat gaping, party hats perched comically on their heads. Waiters froze, huge trays of pasta quivering on their splayed fingers. Chubby Italian infants covered their eyes with chubby fingers. It was always like this in the beginning: the shocked silence. Then came the screaming.

A wine bottle crashed to the floor. It broke the spell. The pandemonium started. Holly winced. Trolls hated noise almost as much as light.

The troll lifted massive shaggy shoulders, its retractable claws sliding out with an ominous *schiiick*. Classic predator behaviour. The beast was about to strike.

Holly drew her weapon and flicked it up to the second setting. She couldn't kill the troll under any circumstances. Not to save humans. But she could certainly put him out until Retrieval arrived.

Aiming for the weak point at the base of the skull, she let the troll have a long burst of the concentrated ion ray. The beast staggered, stumbled a few steps, then got very angry.

It's OK, thought Holly, I'm shielded. Invisible. To any

onlookers it would seem as though the pulsing blue beam emanated from thin air.

The troll rounded on her, its muddy dreadlocks swinging like candles.

No panic. It can't see me.

The troll picked up a table.

Invisible. Totally invisible.

He pulled back a shaggy arm and let fly.

Just a slight shimmer in the air.

The table tumbled straight towards her head.

Holly moved. A second too late. The table clipped her backpack, knocking the petrol tank clean off. It span through the air, trailing flammable fluid.

Italian restaurants – wouldn't you know it – full of candles. The tank twirled right through an elaborate candelabrum. It burst into flames, like some deadly firework. Most of the petrol landed on the troll. So did Holly.

The troll could see her. There was no doubt about it. It squinted at her through the hated light, its brow a rictus of pain and fear. Her shield was off. Her magic had gone.

Holly twisted in the troll's grip, but it was useless. The creature's fingers were the size of bananas, but nowhere near as pliant. They were squashing the breath from her ribcage with savage ease. Needle-like claws were scraping at the toughened material of her uniform. Any second now, they would punch through, and that would be that.

Holly couldn't think. The restaurant was a carousel of chaos. The troll was gnashing its tusks; greasy molars trying to grip her helmet. Holly could smell its fetid breath through her filters. She could smell the odour of burning fur too, as the fire spread along the troll's back.

The beast's green tongue rasped across her visor, sliming the lower section. The visor! That was it. Her only chance. Holly wormed her free hand to the helmet controls. The tunnel lights. High beams.

She depressed the sunken button and 800 watts of unfiltered light blasted from the twin spotlights above her eyes.

The troll reared back, a penetrating scream exploding from between rows of teeth. Dozens of glasses and bottles shattered where they stood. It was too much for the poor beast. Stunned, set on fire and now blinded. The shock and pain made their way through to its tiny brain, ordering it to shut down. The troll complied, keeling over with almost comical stiffness. Holly rolled to avoid a scything tusk.

There was complete silence, but for tinkling glass, crackling fur and the sudden release of breath. Holly climbed shakily to her feet. There were a lot of eyes following her — human eyes. She was 100 per cent visible. And these humans wouldn't stay complacent for long. This breed never did. Containment was the issue.

She raised her empty palms. A gesture of peace.

'*Scusatemi tutti*,' she said, the language flowing easily from her tongue.

The Italians, ever graceful, muttered that it was nothing.

Holly reached slowly into her pocket and withdrew a small sphere. She placed it in the middle of the floor.

'*Guardate*,' she said. Look.

The restaurant's patrons complied, leaning in to see the small silver ball. It was ticking, faster and faster, almost like a countdown. Holly turned her back to the sphere. Three, two, one …

Boom! Flash! Mass unconsciousness. Nothing fatal, but headaches all around in about forty minutes. Holly sighed. Safe. For the moment. She ran to the door and slid the latch across. Nobody was going in or out. Except through the big gaping hole in the wall. Next she doused the smouldering troll with the contents of the restaurant's fire extinguisher, hoping the icy powder wouldn't revive the sleeping behemoth.

Holly surveyed the mess she had created. There was no doubt, it was a shambles. Worse than Hamburg. Root would skin her alive. She'd rather face the troll any day. This was the end of her career for sure, but suddenly that didn't seem so important because her ribs were aching and she had a blinder of a pressure headache coming on. Perhaps a rest, just for a second, so she could pull herself together before Retrieval showed up.

Holly didn't even bother looking for a chair. She simply allowed her legs to buckle beneath her, sinking to the chessboard lino floor.

Waking up to Commander Root's bulging features is the stuff of nightmares. Holly's eyes flickered open, and for a second she could have sworn that there was concern in those eyes. But then it was gone, replaced by the customary vein-popping fury.

'Captain Short!' he roared, mindless of her headache. 'What in the name of sanity happened here?'

Holly rose shakily to her feet.

'I … That is … There was …' The sentences just wouldn't come.

'You disobeyed a direct order. I told you to hang back! You know it's forbidden to enter a human building without an invitation.'

Holly shook the shadows from her vision.

'I got invited in. A child called for help.'

'You're on shaky ground there, Short.'

'There is precedent, sir. Corporal Rowe versus the State. The jury ruled that the trapped woman's cry for help could be accepted as an invitation into the building. Anyway, you're all here now. That means you accepted the invitation too.'

'Hmm,' said Root doubtfully. 'I suppose you were lucky. Things could have been worse.'

Holly looked around. Things couldn't have been a lot worse. The establishment was pretty trashed and there were forty humans out for the count. The tech boys were attaching mind-wipe electrodes to the temples of unconscious diners.

'We managed to secure the area, in spite of half the town hammering on the door.'

'What about the hole?'

Root smirked. 'See for yourself.'

Holly glanced over. Retrieval had jimmied a hologram lead into the existing electricity sockets and were projecting an unbattered wall over the hole. The holograms were handy for quick patches, but no good under scrutiny. Anyone who examined the wall too closely would have noticed that the slightly transparent patch was exactly the same as the stretch beside it. In this case there were two identical patches of spiderweb cracks and two reproductions of the same Rembrandt. But the people inside the pizzeria were in no condition to examine walls, and by the time they woke up, the wall would have been repaired by the Telekinetic Division and the entire paranormal experience would be removed from their memories.

A Retrieval officer bolted from the restroom.

'Commander!'

'Yes, Sergeant?'

'There's a human in here, sir. The Concusser didn't

reach him. He's coming, sir. Right now, sir!'

'Shields!' barked Root. 'Everyone!'

Holly tried. She really did. But it wouldn't come. Her magic was gone. A toddler waddled out of the bathroom, his eyes heavy with sleep. He pointed a pudgy finger directly at Holly.

'*Ciao, folletta*,' he said, before climbing into his father's lap to continue his snooze.

Root shimmered back into the visible spectrum. He was, if possible, even angrier than before.

'What happened to your shield, Short?'

Holly swallowed.

'Stress, Commander,' she offered hopefully.

Root wasn't having any of it. 'You lied to me, Captain. You're not running hot at all, are you?'

Holly shook her head mutely.

'How long since you completed the Ritual?'

Holly chewed her lip. 'I'd say … about … four years, sir.'

Root nearly popped a vein.

'Four … Four years? It's a wonder you lasted this long! Do it now. Tonight! You're not coming below ground again without your powers. You're a danger to yourself and your fellow officers!'

'Yessir.'

'Get a set of Hummingbirds from Retrieval and zip across to the old country. There's a full moon tonight.'

'Yessir.'

'And don't think I've forgotten about this shambles. We'll talk about it when you get back.'

'Yessir. Very good, sir.'

Holly turned to go, but Root cleared his throat for attention.

'Oh, and Captain Short ...'

'Yessir?'

Root's face had lost its purple tinge and he almost seemed embarrassed.

'Well done on the life-saving thing. Could have been worse, an awful lot worse.'

Holly beamed behind her visor. Perhaps she wouldn't be kicked out of Recon after all.

'Thank you, sir.'

Root grunted, his complexion returning to its normal ruddy hue.

'Now get out of here, and don't come back until you're full to the tips of your ears with magic!'

Holly sighed. So much for gratitude.

'Yes, sir. On my way, sir.'

CHAPTER 4: **ABDUCTION**

 ARTEMIS'S main problem was one of location – how to locate a leprechaun. This was one sly bunch of fairies, hanging around for God knows how many millennia and still not one photo, not one frame of video. Not even a Loch-Ness-type hoax. They weren't exactly a sociable group. And they were smart too. No one had ever got his hands on fairy gold. But no one had ever had access to the Book either. And puzzles were so simple when you had the key.

Artemis had summoned the Butlers to his study, and spoke to them now from behind a mini-lectern.

'There are certain rituals every fairy must complete to renew his magic,' explained Artemis.

Butler and Juliet nodded, as though this were a normal briefing.

Artemis flicked through his hard copy of the Book and selected a passage.

'From the earth thine power flows,

Given through courtesy, so thanks are owed.

Pluck thou the magick seed,

Where full moon, ancient oak and twisted water meet.

And bury it far from where it was found,

So return your gift into the ground.'

Artemis closed the text. 'Do you see?'

Butler and Juliet kept nodding, while still looking thoroughly mystified.

Artemis sighed. 'The leprechaun is bound by certain rituals. Very specific rituals, I might add. We can use them to track one down.'

Juliet raised a hand, even though she herself was four years Artemis's senior.

'Yes?'

'Well, the thing is, Artemis,' she said hesitantly, twisting a strand of blonde hair in a way that several of the local louts considered extremely attractive. 'The bit about leprechauns.'

Artemis frowned. It was a bad sign. 'Your point, Juliet?'

'Well, leprechauns. You know they're not real, don't you?'

Butler winced. It was his fault really. He'd never got around to filling in his sister on the mission parameters.

Artemis scowled reprovingly at him.

'Butler hasn't already talked to you about this?'

'No. Was he supposed to?'

'Yes, he certainly was. Perhaps he thought you'd laugh at him.'

Butler squirmed. That was exactly what he'd thought. Juliet was the only person alive who laughed at him with embarrassing regularity. Most other people did it once. Just once.

Artemis cleared his throat. 'Let us proceed under the assumption that the fairy folk do exist and that I am not a gibbering moron.'

Butler nodded weakly. Juliet was unconvinced.

'Very well. Now, as I was saying, the People have to fulfil a specific ritual to renew their powers. According to my interpretation, they must pick a seed from an ancient oak tree by the bend in a river. And they must do this during the full moon.'

The light began to dawn in Butler's eyes. 'So all we have to do ...'

'Is run a cross-reference through the weather satellites, which I already have. Believe it or not, there aren't that many ancient oaks left, if you take ancient to be a hundred years plus. When you factor in the river bend and full moon, there are precisely one hundred and twenty-nine sites to be surveyed in this country.'

Butler grinned. Stakeout. Now the Master was talking his language.

'There are preparations to be made for our guest's

arrival,' said Artemis, handing a typewritten sheet of A4 to Juliet. 'These alterations must be made to the cellar. See to it, Juliet. To the letter.'

'Yes, Arty.'

Artemis frowned, but only slightly. For reasons that he couldn't quite fathom, he didn't mind terribly when Juliet called him by the pet name his mother had for him.

Butler scratched his chin thoughtfully. Artemis noticed the gesture.

'Query?'

'Well, Artemis. The sprite in Ho Chi Minh City ...'

Artemis nodded. 'I know. Why didn't we simply abduct her?'

'Yes, sir.'

'According to Chi Lun's *Almanac of the People*, a seventh-century manuscript recovered from the lost city of Sh'shamo: "Once a fairy has taken spirits with the Mud People" – that's us, by the way – "they are forever dead to their brothers and sisters." So there was no guarantee that that particular fairy was worth even an ounce of gold. No, my old friend, we need fresh blood. All clear?'

Butler nodded.

'Good. Now, there are several items you will need to procure for our moonlight jaunts.'

Butler scanned the sheet: basic field equipment, a few eyebrow raisers, nothing too puzzling until ...

'Sunglasses? At night?'

When Artemis smiled, as he did now, one almost expected vampire fangs to sprout from his gums.

'Yes, Butler. Sunglasses. Trust me.'

And Butler did. Implicitly.

Holly activated the thermal coil in her suit and climbed to 4,000 metres. The Hummingbird wings were top of the range. The battery readout showed four red bars – more than enough for a quick jaunt through mainland Europe and across the British Isles. Of course, the regulations said always travel over water if possible, but Holly could never resist knocking the snowcap from the highest alp on her way past.

The suit protected Holly from the worst of the elements, but she could still feel the chill sinking into her bones. The moon seemed huge from this altitude, the craters on its surface easily distinguishable. Tonight it was a perfect sphere. A magical full moon. Immigration would have their hands full, as thousands of surface-sick fairies were drawn irresistibly overground. A large percentage would make it, probably causing mayhem in their revelry. The earth's mantle was riddled with illegal tunnels and it was impossible to police them all.

Holly followed the Italian coast up to Monaco and from there across the Alps to France. She loved flying, all fairies did. According to the Book, they had once been equipped with wings of their own, but evolution had stripped them of this power. All but the sprites. One school of thought believed that the People were descended from airborne dinosaurs. Possibly pterodactyls. Much of the upper-body skeletal structure was the same. This theory would certainly explain the tiny nub of bone on each shoulder blade.

Holly toyed with the idea of visiting Disneyland Paris. The LEP had several undercover operatives stationed there, most of them working in the Snow White exhibit. It was one of the few places on earth that the People could pass unnoticed. But if some tourist got a photo of her and it ended up on the Internet, Root would have her badge for sure. With a sigh of regret, she passed over the shower of multicoloured fireworks below.

Once over the Channel, Holly flew low, skipping over the white-crested waves. She called out to the dolphins and they rose to the surface, leaping from the water to match her pace. She could see the pollution in them, bleaching their skin white and causing red sores on their backs. And although she smiled, her heart was breaking. Mud People had a lot to answer for.

Finally the coast loomed ahead of her. The old country. Éiriú, the land where time began. The most magical place on the planet. It was here, 10,000 years ago, that the ancient fairy race, the Dé Danann, had battled against the demon Fomorians, carving the famous Giant's Causeway with the strength of their magical blasts. It was here that the Lia Fáil stood, the rock at the centre of the universe, where the fairy kings and later the human Ard Rí were crowned. And it was also here, unfortunately, that the Mud People were most in tune with magic, which resulted in a far higher People-sighting rate than you got anywhere else on the planet. Thankfully the rest of the world assumed that the Irish were crazy, a theory that the Irish themselves did nothing to debunk. They had somehow got it into their heads that each fairy lugged around a pot of gold with them wherever they went. While it was true that LEP had a ransom fund, because of its officers' high-risk occupation, no human had ever taken a chunk of it yet. This didn't stop the Irish population in general from skulking around rainbows, hoping to win the supernatural lottery.

But in spite of all that, if there was one race the People felt an affinity for it was the Irish. Perhaps it was their eccentricity, perhaps their dedication to the *craic*, as they called it. And if the People were actually related to humans, as another theory had it, odds on it was the Emerald Isle where it started.

Holly punched up a map on her wrist locator and set it to sweep for magical hotspots. The best site would obviously be Tara, near the Lia Fáil, but on a night like tonight, every traditionalist fairy with an overground pass would be dancing around the holy scene, so best to give it a miss.

There was a secondary site not far from here, just off the south-east coast. Easy access from the air, but remote and desolate for land-bound humans. Holly reined in the throttle and descended to eighty metres. She skipped over a bristling evergreen forest, emerging in a moonlit meadow. A silver thread of river bisected the field and there, nestling in the fold of a meander loop, was the proud oak.

Holly checked her locator for life forms. Once she judged the cow two fields over not to be a threat, she cut her engines and glided to the foot of the mighty tree.

Four months of stakeout. Even Butler, the consummate professional, was beginning to dread the long nights of damp and insect bites. Thankfully, the moon was not full every night.

It was always the same. They would crouch in their foil-lined hide in complete silence, Butler repeatedly checking his equipment, while Artemis stared unblinking through the eye of the scope. At times like these, nature seemed deafening in their confined space. Butler longed to whistle, to make conversation, anything to break the unnatural silence. But Artemis's concentration was absolute. He would brook no interference or lapse of focus. This was business.

Tonight they were in the south-east. The most inaccessible site yet. Butler had been forced to make three trips to the jeep in order to hump the equipment across a stile, a bog and two fields. His boots and trousers were ruined. And now he would have to sit in the hide with ditchwater soaking into the seat of his trousers. Artemis had somehow contrived to remain spotless.

The hide was ingenious in design and interest had already been expressed in the manufacturing rights – mostly by military representatives – but Artemis had resolved to sell the patent to a sporting-goods multinational. It was constructed of an elasticated foil polymer on a multi-hinged fibreglass skeleton. The foil, similar to that used by NASA, trapped the heat inside the structure while preventing the camouflaged outside surface from overheating. This ensured that any animals sensitive to heat would be unaware of its presence. The hinges meant that the hide would move almost like a liquid, filling whatever depression it was dropped into. Instant shelter and vantage point. You simply placed the Velcroed bag in a hole and pulled the string.

But all the cleverness in the world couldn't improve the atmosphere. Something was troubling Artemis. It was plain in the web of premature lines that spread from the corners of his deep-blue eyes.

After several nights of fruitless surveillance, Butler plucked up enough courage to ask …

'Artemis,' he began hesitantly, 'I realize it's not my place, but I know there's something wrong. And if there's anything I can do to help ...'

Artemis didn't speak for several moments. And for those few moments, Butler saw the face of a young boy. The boy Artemis might have been.

'It's my mother, Butler,' he said at last. 'I'm beginning to wonder if she'll ever –'

Then the proximity alarm flashed red.

Holly hooked the wings over a low branch, unstrapping the helmet to give her ears some air. You had to be careful with elfin ears – a few hours in the helmet and they started to flake. She gave the tips a massage. No dry skin there. That was because she had a daily moisturizing regime, not like some of the male LEP officers. When they took off their helmets, you'd swear it had just started to snow.

Holly paused for a minute to admire the view. Ireland certainly was picturesque. Even the Mud People hadn't been able to destroy that. Not yet anyway ... Give them another century or two. The river was folding gently before her like a silver snake, hissing as the water tumbled across a stony bed. The oak tree crackled overhead, its branches rasping together in the bracing breeze.

Now, to work. She could do the tourist thing all night once her business was complete. A seed. She needed a seed. Holly bent to the ground, brushing the dried leaves and twigs from the clay's surface. Her fingers closed around a smooth acorn. That wasn't hard now, was it? she thought. All that remained for her to do was plant it somewhere else and her powers would come rushing back.

Butler checked the porta-radar, muting the volume in case the equipment betrayed their position. The red arm swept the screen with agonizing lethargy, and then … *Flash!* An upright figure by the tree. Too small for an adult, the wrong proportions for a child. He gave Artemis the thumbs-up. Possible match.

Artemis nodded, strapping the mirrored sunglasses across his brow. Butler followed his lead, popping the cap on his weapon's starlight scope. This was no ordinary dart rifle. It had been specially tooled for a Kenyan ivory hunter and had the range and rapid-fire capacity of a Kalashnikov. Butler had picked it up for a song from a government official after the ivory poacher's execution.

They crept into the night with practised silence. The diminutive figure before them unhooked a contraption from around its shoulders and lifted a full-face helmet from a definitely non-human head. Butler wrapped the rifle strap twice around his wrist, pulling the stock into his shoulder. He activated the scope and a red dot appeared in the centre of the figure's back. Artemis nodded and his manservant squeezed the trigger.

In spite of a million to one odds, it was at that precise moment that the figure bent low to the earth.

⋃⍟⏉ ⟶ ⁓⍟⏉⍙⌐ ⬡⍥⏃⏃ ⬥◑⍥⟊⍦ ⬡⍟

*

Something whizzed over Holly's head, something that glinted in the starlight. Holly had enough on-the-job experience to realize that she was under fire, and immediately curled her elfin frame into a ball, minimizing the target.

She drew her pistol, rolling towards the shelter of the tree trunk. Her brain scrambled for possibilities. Who could be shooting at her and why?

Something was waiting beside the tree. Something roughly the size of a mountain, but considerably more mobile.

'Nice pea-shooter,' grinned the figure, smothering Holly's gun hand in a turnip-sized fist.

Holly managed to extricate her fingers a nanosecond before they snapped like brittle spaghetti.

'I don't suppose you would consider peaceful surrender?' said a cold voice behind her.

Holly turned, elbows raised for combat.

'No,' sighed the boy melodramatically. 'I suppose not.'

Holly put on her best brave face.

'Stay back, human. You don't know what you're dealing with.'

The boy laughed. 'I believe, fairy, that you are the one unfamiliar with the facts.'

Fairy? He knew she was a fairy.

'I have magic mud-worm. Enough to turn you and

your gorilla into pig droppings.'

The boy took a step closer. 'Brave words, miss. But lies nonetheless. If, as you say, you had magic, you would have no doubt used it by now. No, I suspect that you have gone too long without the Ritual and you are here to replenish your powers.'

Holly was dumbfounded. There was a human before her, casually spouting sacred secrets. This was disastrous. Catastrophic. It could mean the end of generations of peace. If the humans were aware of a fairy subculture, it was only a matter of time before the two species went to war. She must do something, and there was only one weapon left in her arsenal.

The *mesmer* is the lowest form of magic and requires only a trickle of power. There are even certain humans with a bent for the talent. It is within the ability of even the most drained fairy to put a complete mind kibosh on any human alive.

Holly summoned the final dribble of magic from the base of her skull.

'Human,' she intoned, her voice suddenly resonating with bass tones, 'your will is mine.'

Artemis smiled, safe behind his mirrored lenses. 'I doubt it,' he said, and nodded curtly.

Holly felt the dart puncture the suit's toughened material, depositing its load of curare and succinylcholine chloride-based tranquillizer into her shoulder. The world instantly dissolved into a series of technicoloured bubbles and, try as she might, Holly couldn't seem to hold on to more than one thought. And that thought was: how did they know? It spiralled around her head as she sank into unconsciousness. How did they know? How did they know? How did they ...

Artemis saw the pain in the creature's eyes as the hollow hypodermic plunged into her body. And for a moment he experienced misgivings. A female. He hadn't expected that. A female, like Juliet, or Mother. Then the moment passed and he was himself again.

'Good shooting,' he said, bending to study their prisoner. Definitely a girl. Pretty too. In a pointy sort of way.

'Sir?'

'Hmm?'

Butler was pointing to the creature's helmet. It was half-buried in a drift of leaves where the fairy had dropped it. A buzzing noise was coming from the crown.

Artemis picked up the contraption by the straps, searching for the source.

'Ah, here we are.' He plucked the viewcam from its slot, careful to point the lens away from him. 'Fairy technology. Most impressive,' he muttered, popping the battery from its groove. The camera whined and died. 'Nuclear power source, if I'm not mistaken. We must be careful not to underestimate our opponents.'

Butler nodded, sliding their captive into an oversized duffel bag. Something else to be lugged across two fields, a bog and a stile.

CHAPTER 5: MISSING IN ACTION

COMMANDER Root was sucking on a particularly noxious fungus cigar. Several of the Retrieval Squad had nearly passed out in the shuttle. Even the pong from the manacled troll seemed mild in comparison. Of course, no one said anything, their boss being touchier than a septic bum boil.

Foaly, on the other hand, delighted in antagonizing his superior. 'None of your rancid stogies in here, Commander!' he brayed, the moment Root made it back to Ops. 'The computers don't like smoke!'

Root scowled, certain that Foaly was making this up. Nevertheless, the commander was not prepared to risk a computer crash in the middle of an alert and so doused his cigar in the coffee cup of a passing gremlin.

'Now, Foaly, what's this so-called alert? And it better be good this time!'

The centaur had a tendency to go completely hyper over trivialities. He'd once gone to Defcon Two because his human satellite stations were out.

'It's good all right,' Foaly assured him. 'Or should I say bad? Very bad.'

Root felt the ulcer in his gut begin to bubble like a volcano.

'How bad?'

Foaly punched up Ireland on the Eurosat. 'We lost contact with Captain Short.'

'Why am I not surprised?' groaned Root, burying his face in his hands.

'We had her all the way over the Alps.'

'The Alps? She took a land route?'

Foaly nodded. 'Against regulations, I know. But everyone does it.'

The commander agreed grudgingly. Who could resist a view like that? As a rookie, he'd been placed on report himself for that exact offence.

'OK. Move on. When did we lose her?'

Foaly opened a VT box on the screen.

'This is the feed from Holly's helmet unit. Here we are over Disneyland Paris ...'

The centaur pressed the fast-forward.

'Now dolphins, blah blah blah. The Irish coastline. Still no worries. Look, her locator comes into shot. Captain Short is scanning for magic hotspots. Site fifty-seven shows up red, so she heads for that one.'

'Why not Tara?'

Foaly snorted. 'Tara? Every fairy hippie in the northern hemisphere will be dancing around the Lia Fáil at the full moon. There'll be so many shields on, it'll look like the whole place is under water.'

'Fine,' grunted Root through gritted teeth. 'Just get on with it, will you.'

' All right. Don't get your ears in a knot.' Foaly skipped several minutes of tape. 'Now. Here's the interesting bit … Nice smooth landing, hangs up the wings. Holly takes off the helmet.'

'Against regulations,' interjected Root. 'LEP officers must never remove –'

'LEP officers must never remove their headgear above ground, unless said headgear is defective,' completed Foaly. 'Yes, Commander, we all know what the handbook says. But are you trying to tell me that you never sneaked a breath of air after a few hours in the sky?'

'No,' admitted Root. 'What are you? Her fairy godmother or something? Get to the important bit!'

Foaly smirked behind his hand. Driving up Root's blood pressure was one of the few perks of the job. No one else would dare to do it. That was because everybody else was replaceable. Not Foaly. He'd built the system from scratch and if anyone else even tried to boot it up, a hidden virus would bring it crashing about their pointy ears.

'The important bit. Here we are. Look. Suddenly Holly drops the helmet. It must land lens down because we lose picture. We've still got sound though, so I'll bring that up.'

Foaly boosted the audio signal, filtering out background noise.

'Not great quality. The mike is in the camera. So that was nose down in the dirt too.'

'Nice pea-shooter,' said a voice. Definitely human. Deep too. That usually meant big.

Root raised an eyebrow. 'Pea-shooter?'

'Slang for gun.'

'Oh.' Then the importance of that simple statement struck him. 'She drew her weapon.'

'Just wait. It gets worse.'

'I don't suppose you would consider peaceful surrender?' said a second voice. Just listening to it gave the commander shivers. 'No,' continued the voice. 'I suppose not.'

'This is bad,' said Root, his face uncharacteristically pale. 'This feels like a set-up. These two goons were waiting. How is that possible?'

Holly's voice came through the speaker then, typically brazen in the face of danger. The commander sighed. At least she was alive. It was more bad news though as the parties exchanged threats, and the second human displayed an uncommon knowledge of fairy affairs.

'He knows about the Ritual!'

'Here's the worst bit.'

Root's jaw dropped. 'The worst bit?'

Holly's voice again. This time layered with the *mesmer*.

'Now she has them,' crowed Root.

But apparently not. Not only did the *mesmer* prove ineffective, but the mysterious pair seemed to find it amusing.

'That's all there is from Holly,' noted Foaly. 'One of the Mud People messes around with the camera for a bit and then we lose everything.'

Root rubbed the creases between his eyes. 'Not much to go on. No visual, not even a name. We can't really be a hundred per cent sure that we have a situation.'

'You want proof?' asked Foaly, rewinding the tape. 'I'll give you proof.'

He ran the available video.

'Now watch this. I'm going to slow it right down. One frame per second.'

Root leaned in close to the screen, close enough to see the pixels.

'Captain Short comes in for a landing. She takes off her helmet. Bends down, presumably to pick up an acorn, and … there!'

Foaly jabbed the pause button, freezing the picture completely. 'See anything unusual?'

The commander felt his ulcer churn into overdrive. Something had appeared in the top right-hand corner of the frame. At first glance it seemed like a shaft of light, but light from what or reflected from what?

'Can you blow that up?'

'No problem.'

Foaly cut to the relevant area, increasing it by 400 per cent. The light expanded to fill the screen.

'Oh no,' breathed Root.

There on the monitor before them, in frozen suspension, was a hypodermic dart. There could be no doubt. Captain Holly Short was missing in action. Most probably dead, but at the very least held captive by a hostile force.

'Tell me we still have the locator.'

'Yep. Strong signal. Moving north at about eighty klicks an hour.'

Root was silent for a moment, formulating his strategy.

'Go to full alert, and get Retrieval out of their bunks and back down here. Prep them for a surface shot. I want full tactical and a couple of techies. You too, Foaly. We may have to stop time on this one.'

'Ten four, Commander. You want Recon in on this?'

Root nodded. 'You bet.'

'I'll call in Captain Vein. He's our number one.'

'Oh no,' said Root. 'For a job like this, we need our very best. And that's me. I'm reactivating myself.'

Foaly was so amazed, he couldn't even formulate a smart comment.

'You're ... You're ...'

'Yes, Foaly. Don't act so surprised. I have more successful recons under my belt than any officer in history. Plus I did my basic training in Ireland. Back in the top hat and shillelagh days.'

'Yes, but that was five hundred years ago, and you were no spring bud then, not to put too fine a point on it.'

Root smiled dangerously. 'Don't worry, Foaly. I'm still running red hot. And I'll make up for my age with a really big gun. Now get a pod ready. I'm leaving on the next flare.'

Foaly did what he was told without a single quip. When the commander got that glint in his eyes, you hopped to and kept your mouth shut. But there was another reason for Foaly's silent compliance. It had just hit him that Holly could be in real trouble. Centaurs don't make many friends and Foaly was worried he might lose one of the few he had.

Artemis had anticipated some technological advances, but nothing like the treasure trove of fairy hardware spread out on the four-wheel drive's dashboard.

'Impressive,' he murmured. 'We could abort this mission right now and still make a fortune in patents.'

Artemis ran a hand-held scanner bar over the

unconscious elf's wristband. He then fed the fairy characters into his PowerBook translator.

'This is a locator of some kind. No doubt this leprechaun's comrades are tracking us right now.'

Butler swallowed. 'Right now, sir?'

'It would seem so. Or at any rate they're tracking the locator —'

Artemis stopped speaking suddenly, his eyes losing focus as the electricity in his cranium sparked off another brainwave.

'Butler?'

The manservant felt his pulse quicken. He knew that tone. Something was afoot.

'Yes, Artemis?'

'That Japanese whaler. The one seized by the port authorities. Is she still tied up at the docks?'

Butler nodded. 'Yes, I believe so.'

Artemis twirled the locator's band around his index finger.

'Good. Take us down there. I believe it's time to let our diminutive friends know exactly who they're dealing with.'

Root rubber-stamped his own reactivation with remarkable speed – very unusual for LEP upper management. Generally it took months, and several mind-crushingly dull meetings, to approve any application to the Recon Squad. Luckily, Root had a bit of influence with the commander.

It felt good to be back in a field uniform and Root even managed to convince himself that the jumpsuit was no tighter around the middle than it used to be. The bulge, he rationalized, was caused by all the new equipment they jammed into these things. Personally, Root had no time for gadgetry. The only items the commander was interested in were the wings on his back and the multi-phase, water-cooled, tri-barrelled blaster strapped to his hip – the most powerful production handgun under the world. Old, to be sure, but it had seen Root through a dozen fire fights and it made him feel like a field officer again.

The nearest chute to Holly's position was E1:Tara. Not exactly an ideal location for a stealth mission, but with barely two hours of moon time left there was no time for an overground jaunt. If there was to be any chance of sorting out this mess before sunrise, speed was of the essence. He commandeered the E1 shuttle for his team, bumping a tour group who had apparently been queuing for two years.

'Tough nuggets,' Root growled at the holiday rep. 'And what's more, I'm shutting down all non-essential flights until the present crisis is past.'

'And when might that be?' squeaked the irate gnome, brandishing a notebook as though she were prepared to make a complaint of some kind.

Root spat out the butt of his cigar, squashing it comprehensively beneath his boot heel. The symbolism was all too obvious.

'The chutes will be opened, madam, when I feel like it,' growled the commander. 'And if you and your fluorescent uniform don't get out of my way, I'll yank your operating licence and have you thrown into the cells for obstructing an LEP officer.'

The holiday rep wilted before him and slunk back into line, wishing her uniform wasn't quite so pink.

Foaly was waiting at the pod. Serious though the moment was, he couldn't resist an amused whinny at the sight of Root's belly wobbling ever so slightly in his clinging jumpsuit.

'Are you sure about this, Commander? Generally we allow only one passenger per pod.'

'What do you mean?' snarled Root. 'There is only one ...'

Then he caught Foaly's meaningful glance at his stomach.

'Oh. Ha ha. Very amusing. Keep it up, Foaly. I have my limit, you know.'

But it was a hollow threat and they both knew it. Not only had Foaly built their communications network from scratch, but he was also a pioneer in the field of flare prediction. Without him, human technology could very easily catch up with the fairy brand.

Root strapped himself into the pod. No half-century-old crafts for the commander. This baby was fresh off the assembly line. All silver and shiny, with the new jagged fin stabilizers that were supposed to read the magma currents automatically. Foaly's innovation, of course. For a century or so his pod designs had leaned towards the futuristic – plenty of neon and rubber. Lately, however, his sensibilities had become more retrospective, replacing the gadgetry with walnut dashes and leather upholstery. Root found this old-style decor strangely comforting.

He wrapped his fingers around the joysticks and suddenly realized just how long it was since he had *ridden the hotshots*. Foaly noticed his discomfort.

'Don't worry, chief,' he said without the usual cynicism. 'It's like riding a unicorn. You never forget.'

Root grunted, unconvinced. 'Let's get the show on the road,' he muttered. 'Before I change my mind.'

Foaly hauled the door across until the suction ring took hold, sealing the portal with a pneumatic hiss. Root's face took on a green hue through the quartz pane. He didn't look too scary any more. Quite the opposite in fact.

Artemis was performing a little field surgery on the fairy locator. It was no mean feat to alter some of the dimensions without destroying the mechanisms. The technologies were most definitely incompatible. Imagine trying to perform open-heart surgery with a sledgehammer.

The first problem was opening the cursed thing. The screwheads defied both flathead and Phillips screwdrivers. Even Artemis's extensive set of Allen keys were unable to find purchase in the tiny grooves. Think futuristic, Artemis told himself. Think advanced technology.

It came to him after a few moments' silent contemplation. Magnetic bolts. Obvious really. But how to construct a revolving magnetic field in the back of a four-wheel drive? Impossible. The only thing for it was to chase the screws around manually with a domestic magnet.

Artemis hunted the small magnet from its niche in the toolbox and applied both poles to the tiny screws. The negative side wiggled them slightly. It was enough to give Artemis some purchase with needlenose pliers, and he soon had the locator's panel disassembled before him.

The circuitry was minute. And not a sign of a solder bead. They must use another form of binder. Perhaps if he had time the principles of this device could be unravelled, but for now he would have to improvise. He would have to rely on the inattention of others. And if the People were anything like humans, they saw what they wanted to see.

Artemis held the locator's face up to the cab's light. It

was translucent. Slightly polarized but good enough. He nudged a slew of tiny shimmering wires aside, inserting a buttonhole camera in the space. He secured the pea-sized transmitter with a dab of silicone. Crude but effective. Hopefully.

The magnetic screws refused to be coaxed back into their grooves without the proper tool, so Artemis was forced to glue them too. Messy, but it should suffice, provided the locator wasn't examined too closely. And if it was? Well, he would only lose an advantage that he never expected to have in the first place.

Butler knocked off his high beams as they entered the city limits. 'Docks coming up, Artemis,' he said over his shoulder. 'There's bound to be a Customs and Excise crew around somewhere.'

Artemis nodded. It made sense. The port was a thriving artery of illegal activity. Over fifty per cent of the country's contraband made it ashore somewhere along this half-mile stretch.

'A diversion then, Butler. Two minutes are all I need.'

The manservant nodded thoughtfully.

'The usual?'

'I don't see why not. Knock yourself out … Or rather don't.'

Artemis blinked. That was his second joke in recent times. And his first aloud. Better take care. This was no time for frivolity.

*

The dockers were rolling cigarettes. It wasn't easy with fingers the size of lead bars, but they managed. And if a few strands of brown tobacco dropped to the rough flagstones, what of it? The pouches were available by the carton from a little man who didn't bother adding government tax to his prices.

Butler strolled over to the men, his eyes shadowed beneath the brim of a watch cap.

'Cold night,' he said to the assembled group.

No one replied. Policemen came in all shapes and sizes.

The big stranger persevered. 'Even work is better than standing around on a frosty one like tonight.'

One of the workmen, a bit soft in the head, couldn't help nodding in agreement. A comrade drove an elbow into his ribs.

'Still though,' continued the newcomer, 'I don't suppose you girls ever did a decent day's work in your lives.'

Again there was no reply. But this time it was because the dockers' mouths were hanging open in amazement.

'Yep, you're a pathetic-looking bunch, right enough,' went on Butler blithely. 'Oh, I've no doubt you would have passed as men during the famine. But by today's standards you're little more than a pack of blouse-wearing weaklings.'

'Arrrrgh,' said one of the dock hands. It was all he could manage.

92

Butler raised an eyebrow. 'Argh? Pathetic and inarticulate. Nice combination. Your mothers must be so proud.'

The stranger had crossed a sacred line. He had mentioned the men's mothers. Nothing could get him out of a beating now, even the fact that he was obviously a simpleton. Albeit a simpleton with a good vocabulary.

The men stamped out their cigarettes and spread slowly into a semi-circle. It was six against one. You had to feel sorry for them. Butler wasn't finished yet.

'Now before we get into anything, ladies, no scratching, no spitting and no tattling to mummy.'

It was the last straw. The men howled and attacked as one. If they had been paying any attention to their adversary in that moment before contact, they might have noticed that he shifted his weight to lower his centre of gravity. They might also have seen that the hands he drew out of his pockets were the size and approximate shape of spades. But no one was paying attention to Butler – too busy watching their comrades, making sure they weren't alone in the assault.

The thing about a diversion is that it has to be diverting. Big. Crude. Not Butler's style at all. He would have preferred to take these gentlemen out from 500 metres with a dart rifle. Failing that, if contact was absolutely necessary, a series of thumb jabs to the nerve cluster at the base of the neck would be his chosen modus operandi – quiet as a whisper. But that would be defeating the purpose of the exercise.

And so Butler went against his training, screaming like a demon and utilizing the most vulgar combat actions. Vulgar they may have been, but that's not to say they weren't effective. Perhaps a Shao Lin priest could have anticipated some of the more exaggerated movements, but these men were hardly trained adversaries. In fairness, they weren't even completely sober.

Butler dropped the first with a roundhouse punch. Two more had their heads clapped together, cartoon style. The fourth was, to Butler's eternal shame, dispatched with a spinning kick. But the most ostentatious was saved for the last pair. The manservant rolled on to his back, caught them by the collars of their donkey jackets and flipped them into Dublin harbour. Big splashes, plenty of wailing. Perfect.

Two headlights poked from the black shadow of a cargo container and a government saloon screeched along the quay. As anticipated, a Customs and Excise team on stakeout. Butler grinned with grim satisfaction and ducked around the corner. He was long gone before the agents had flipped their badges or begun inquiries. Not that their interrogations would yield much. 'Big as a house' was hardly an adequate description to track him down.

By the time Butler reached the car, Artemis had already returned from his mission.

'Well done, old friend,' he commented. 'Although I'm certain your martial-arts *sensei* is turning in his grave. A spinning kick? How could you?'

Butler bit his tongue, reversing the four-wheel drive off the woodenworks. As they crossed the overpass, he couldn't resist glancing down at the chaos he had created. The government men were hauling a sodden docker from the polluted waters.

Artemis had needed this diversion for something. But Butler knew there was no point in asking what. His employer did not share his plans with anyone until he thought the time was right. And if Artemis Fowl thought the time was right, then it usually was.

Root emerged shaking from the pod. He didn't remember it being like this in his time. Although truth be told, it had probably been an awful lot worse. Back in the shillelagh days, there were no fancy polymer harnesses, no auto thrusters and certainly no external monitors. It was just gut instinct and a touch of enchantment. In some ways Root preferred it like that. Science was taking the magic out of everything.

He stumbled down the tunnel into the terminal. As the number-one preferred destination, Tara had a fully fledged passenger lounge. Six shuttles a week came in from Haven City alone. Not on the flares, of course. Paying tourists didn't like to be jostled around quite that much, unless of course they were on an illegal jaunt to Disneyland.

The fairy fort was crammed with full-moon overnighters complaining about the shuttle suspensions. A beleaguered sprite was sheltering behind her ticket desk, besieged by angry gremlins.

'There's no point hexing me,' squealed the sprite, 'there's the elf you want right there.'

She pointed a quivering green finger at the approaching commander. The gremlin mob turned on Root, and when they saw the triple-barrelled blaster on his hip, they kept right on turning.

Root grabbed the PA stand from behind the desk, and hauled it out to the extent of its cable.

'Now hear this,' he growled, his gravelly tones echoing around the terminal. 'This is Commander Root of the LEP. We have a serious situation above ground and I would appreciate cooperation from all you civilians. First, I would like you all to stop your yapping so I can hear myself think!'

Root paused to make certain his wishes were being respected. They were.

'Secondly, I would like every single one of you, including those squawling infants, to sit down on the courtesy benches until I have gone on my way. Then you can get back to griping or stuffing your faces. Or whatever else it is civilians do.'

No one had ever accused Root of political correctness. No one was ever likely to either.

'And I want whoever's in charge to get over here. Now!'

Root tossed the stand on to the desk. A blare of whistling feedback grated on every eardrum in the building. Within fractions of a second, an out-of-breath elf/goblin hybrid was bobbing at his elbow.

'Anything we can do, Commander?'

Root nodded, twisting a thick cigar into the hole beneath his nose.

'I want you to open a tunnel straight through this place. I don't want to be bothered by Customs or Immigration. Start moving everybody below after my boys get here.'

The shuttle port director swallowed. 'Everybody?'

'Yes. That includes terminal personnel. And take everything you can carry. Full evacuation.' He stopped and glared into the director's mauve eyes. 'This is not a drill.'

'You mean –'

'Yes,' said Root, continuing down the access ramp. 'The Mud People have committed an overtly hostile act. Who knows where this is going?'

The elf/goblin combo watched as Root disappeared in a cloud of cigar smoke. An overtly hostile act? It could mean war. He punched in his accountant's number on his mobile.

'Bark? Yes. This is Nimbus. I want you to sell all my shares in the shuttle port. Yes, all of them. I have a hunch the price is about to take a severe dive.'

Captain Holly Short felt as though a sucker slug was drawing her brain out through her earhole. She tried to figure out what could possibly have caused such agony, but her faculties didn't stretch to memory just yet. Breathing and lying down were about all she could manage.

Time to attempt a word. Something short and pertinent. Help, she decided, would be the one to go for. She took a trembling breath and opened her mouth.

'Mummlp,' said her treacherous lips. No good. Incomprehensible even by a drunken gnome's standards.

What was going on here? She was flat on her back with no more strength in her body than a damp tunnel root. What could have done this to her? Holly concentrated, skirting the edge of blinding pain.

The troll? Was that it? Had the troll mauled her in that restaurant? That would explain a lot. But no. She seemed to remember something about the old country. And the Ritual. And there was something digging into her ankle.

'Hello?'

A voice. Not hers. Not even elfin.

'You awake then?'

One of the European languages. Latin. No, English. She was in England?

'I thought the dart might have killed you. Aliens' insides are different from ours. I saw that on television.'

Gibberish. Aliens, insides? What was the creature talking about?

'You look fit. Like Muchacho Maria, she's a Mexican midget wrestler.'

Holly groaned. Her gift of tongues must be on the blink. Time to see exactly what kind of craziness she was dealing with here. Focusing all her strength at the front of her head, Holly cracked open one eye. She closed it again almost immediately. There appeared to be a giant blonde fly staring down at her.

'Don't be scared,' said the fly. 'Just sunglasses.'

Holly opened both eyes this time. The creature was tapping a silver eye. No, not an eye. A lens. A mirrored lens. Like the lenses worn by the other two ... It all came back in a jolt, rushing to fill the hole in her memory like a combination lock clicking into place. She had been abducted by two humans during the Ritual. Two humans with an extraordinary knowledge of fairy affairs.

Holly tried speaking again. 'Where ... where am I?'

The human giggled delightedly, clapping her hands together. Holly noticed her nails, long and painted.

'You can speak English. What sort of accent is that? Sounds like a little bit of everything.'

Holly frowned. The girl's voice was corkscrewing right

to the middle of her headache. She lifted her arm. No locator.

'Where are my things?'

The girl wagged her finger, as one might at a naughty child.

'Artemis had to take your little gun away, and all those other toys. Couldn't have you hurting yourself.'

'Artemis?'

'Artemis Fowl. This was all his idea. Everything is *always* his idea.'

Holly frowned. *Artemis Fowl*. For some reason, even the name made her shiver. It was a bad omen. Fairy intuition was never wrong.

'They'll come for me, you know,' she said, her voice rasping through dry lips. 'You don't know what you've done.'

The girl frowned. 'You're absolutely right. I have no clue what's going on. So there's no future in trying to psych me out.'

Holly frowned. It was obviously pointless playing mind games with this human. The *mesmer* was her only hope, but that couldn't penetrate reflective surfaces. How the devil did these humans know that? That could be worked out later. For now she had to figure a way to separate this vacuous girl from her mirrored sunglasses.

'You are a pretty human,' she said, voice dripping with honeyed flattery.

'Why, thank you …?'

'Holly.'

'Why, thank you, Holly. I was in the local paper once. I won a competition. Miss Sugar Beet Fair Nineteen-Ninety-Nine.'

'I knew it. Natural beauty. I'll bet your eyes are spectacular.'

'So everyone tells me.' Juliet nodded. 'Lashes like clock springs.'

Holly sighed. 'If only I could see them.'

'Whyever not.'

Juliet's fingers curled around the glasses' arm. Then she hesitated.

'Maybe I shouldn't.'

'Why not? Just for a second.'

'I don't know. Artemis told me never to take these off.'

'He'd never know.'

Juliet pointed to a viewcam mounted on the wall.

'Oh, he'd find out. Artemis finds out about everything.' She leaned in close to the fairy. 'Sometimes I think he can see inside my head too.'

Holly frowned. Foiled again by this Artemis creature.

'Come on. One second. What harm could it do?'

Juliet pretended to think about it. 'None, I suppose. Unless of course you're hoping to nail me with the *mesmer*. Just how stupid do you think I am?'

'I have another idea,' said Holly, her tone altogether

more serious. 'Why don't I get up, knock you out and take those stupid glasses off.'

Juliet laughed delightedly, as if this was the most ridiculous thing she had ever heard.

'Good one, fairy girl.'

'I'm deadly serious, human.'

'Well, if you're serious,' sighed Juliet, reaching a delicate finger behind her lenses to wipe away a tear, 'two reasons. One, Artemis said that while you're in a human dwelling, you have to do what we want. And I want you to stay on that cot.'

Holly closed her eyes. Right again. Where did this group get their information?

'And two.' Juliet smiled again, but this time there was a hint of her brother in those teeth. 'Two, because I went through the same training as Butler, and I've been dying for somebody to practise my piledriver on.'

We'll see about that, human, thought Holly. Captain Short wasn't a hundred per cent yet, and there was also the small matter of the thing digging into her ankle. She thought she knew what it could be, and if she was right, then it could be the beginnings of a plan.

Commander Root had Holly's locator frequency keyed into his helmet face screen. It took Root longer than expected to reach Dublin. The modern wing rigs were more complicated than he was used to, plus he'd neglected to take refresher courses. At the right altitude, he could almost superimpose the luminous map on his visor over the actual Dublin streets below him. Almost.

'Foaly, you pompous centaur,' he barked into his mouthpiece.

'Problem, bossman?' came the tinny reply.

'Problem? You can say that again. When was the last time you updated the Dublin files?'

Root could hear sucking noises in his ear. It sounded as though Foaly was having lunch.

'Sorry, Commander. Just finishing off this carrot. Ahm … Dublin, let's see. Seventy-five … Eighteen seventy-five.'

'I thought so! This place is completely different. The humans have even managed to change the shape of the coastline.'

Foaly was silent for a moment. Root could just imagine him wrestling with the problem. The centaur did not like to be told that any part of his system was out of date.

'OK,' he said at last. 'Here's what I'm going to do. We have a Scope on a satellite TV bird with a footprint in Ireland.'

'I see,' muttered Root, which was basically a lie.

'I'm going to e-mail last week's sweep direct to your visor. Luckily there's a video card in all the new helmets.'

'Luckily.'

'The tricky bit will be to coordinate your flight pattern

with the video feed …'

Root had had enough. 'How long, Foaly?'

'Ahm … Two minutes, give or take.'

'Give or take what?'

'About ten years if my calculations are off.'

'They'd better not be off then. I'll hover until we know.'

One hundred and twenty-four seconds later, Root's black and white blueprints faded out, to be replaced by full-colour daylight imaging. When Root moved it moved, and Holly's locator beacon dot moved too.

'Impressive,' said Root.

'What was that, Commander?'

'I said impressive,' shouted Root. 'No need to get a swollen head.'

The commander heard the sound of a roomful of laughter, and realized that Foaly had him on the speakers. Everyone had heard him complimenting the centaur's work. There'd be no talking to him for at least a month. But it was worth it. The video he was receiving now was bang up to date. If Captain Short was being held in a building, the computer would be able to give him 3D blueprints instantaneously. It was foolproof. Except …

'Foaly, the beacon's gone off shore. What's going on?'

'Boat or ship, sir, I'd say at a guess.'

Root cursed himself for not thinking of it. They'd be having a right old giggle in the situation room. Of course it was a ship. Root dropped down a few hundred metres until its shadowy outline loomed through the mist. A whaler by the looks of it. Technology may have changed over the centuries, but there was still nothing like a harpoon to slaughter the world's largest mammal.

'Captain Short is in there somewhere, Foaly. Below decks. What can you give me?'

'Nothing, sir. It's not a permanent fixture. By the time we've run down her registration, it'd be way too late.'

'What about thermal imaging?'

'No, Commander. That hull must be at least fifty years old. Very high lead content. We can't even penetrate the first layer. I'm afraid you're on your own.'

Root shook his head. 'After all the billions we've poured into your department. Remind me to slash your budget when I get back.'

'Yes, sir,' came the reply, sullen for once. Foaly did not like budget jokes.

'Just have the Retrieval Squad on full alert. I may need them at a moment's notice.'

'I will, sir.'

'You'd better. Over and out.'

Root was on his own. Truth be told, that was the way he liked it. No science. No uppity centaur whinnying in his ear. Just a fairy, his wits and maybe a touch of magic.

Root tilted his polymer wings, hugging the underside of a fogbank. There was no need to be careful. With his shield activated, he was invisible to the human eye. Even on stealth-sensitive radar he would be no more than a barely perceptible distortion. The commander swooped low to the gunwales. It was an ugly craft, this one. The smell of death and pain lingered in the blood-swabbed decks. Many noble creatures had died here, died and been dissected for a few bars of soap and some heating oil. Root shook his head. Humans were such barbarians.

Holly's beeper was flashing urgently now. She was close by. Very close. Somewhere within a 200-metre radius was the hopefully still-breathing form of Captain Short. But without blueprints he would have to navigate the belly of this ship unaided.

Root alighted gently on the deck, his boots adhering slightly to the mixture of dried soap and blubber coating the steel surface. The craft appeared to be deserted. No sentry on the gangplank, no bosun on the bridge, not a light anywhere. Still, no reason to abandon caution. Root knew from bitter experience that humans popped up when you least expected them. Once, when he was helping the Retrieval boys scrape some pod wreckage off a tunnel wall, they were spotted by a group of potholing humans. What a mess that had been. Mass hysteria, high-speed chases, group mind-wipes. The whole nine yards. Root shuddered. Nights like that could put decades on a fairy.

Keeping himself fully shielded, the commander stowed

his wings in their sheath, advancing on foot across the deck. There were no other life forms showing up on his screen but, like Foaly said, the hull had a high lead content; even the paint was lead-based! The entire boat was a floating eco-hazard. The point being that there could be an entire battalion of stormtroopers concealed below decks and his helmetcam would never pick them up. Very reassuring. Even Holly's beacon was a few shades below par, and that had a micro nuclear battery sending out the pulses. Root didn't like this. Not one bit. Keep calm, he derided himself. You're shielded. There's not a human alive that can see you now.

Root hauled open the first hatch. It swung easily enough. The commander sniffed. The Mud People had greased the hinges with whale blubber. Was there no end to their depravity?

The corridor was steeped in viscous darkness, so Root flicked down his infrared filter. OK, so sometimes technology did come in handy, but he wouldn't be telling Foaly that. The maze of pipes and grilling before him was immediately illuminated with an unnatural red light. Minutes later, he was regretting even thinking something nice about the centaur's technology. The infrared filter was messing with his depth perception and he'd whacked his head on two protruding U-bends so far.

Still no sign of life – human or fairy. Plenty of animal. Mostly rodents. And when you're just topping a metre in height yourself, a good-sized rat can be a real threat, especially since rats are one of the few breeds that can see straight through a fairy shield. Root unstrapped his blaster and set it to level three, or *medium rare,* as the elves in the locker room called it. He sent one of the rats scurrying away with a smoking behind as a warning to the rest. Nothing fatal, just enough to teach him not to look sideways at a fairy again in a hurry.

Root picked up his pace. This place was ideal for an ambush. He was virtually blind with his back to the only exit. A Recon nightmare. If one of his own men had pulled a stunt like this, he'd have their stripes for it. But desperate times required judicious risk-taking. That was the essence of command.

He ignored several doors to either side, following the beacon. Ten metres now. A steel hatch sealed the corridor, and Captain Short, or her corpse, lay on the other side of it.

Root put his shoulder to the door. It swung open without protest. Bad news. If a live creature was being held captive, the hatch would be locked. The commander flicked the blaster's power level to five and advanced through the hole. His weapon hummed softly. There was enough power on tap now to vaporize a bull elephant with a single blast.

No sign of Holly. No sign of anything much. He was in a refrigerated storage bay. Glittering stalactites hung from a maze of piping. Root's breath fanned before him in icy clouds. How would that look to a human? Disembodied breathing.

'Ah,' said a familiar voice. 'We have a visitor.'

Root dropped to one knee, levelling the handgun at the voice's source.

'Come to rescue your missing officer, no doubt.'

The commander blinked a bead of sweat from his eye. Sweat? At this temperature?

'Well, I'm afraid you've come to the wrong place.'

The voice was tinny. Artificial. Amplified. Root checked his locator for life signs. There were none. Not in this chamber at any rate. He was being monitored somehow. Was there a camera here somewhere, concealed in the maze of overhead plumbing, that could penetrate the fairy shield?

'Where are you? Show yourself!'

The human chuckled. It echoed unnaturally around the vast hold.

'Oh no. Not yet, my fairy friend. But soon enough. And believe me, when I do, you'll wish I hadn't.'

Root followed the voice. Keep the human talking.

'What do you want?'

'Hmm. What do I want? Again, you will know soon enough.'

There was a low crate in the centre of the hold. On it sat an attaché case. The case was open.

'Why bring me here at all?'

Root poked the case with his pistol. Nothing happened.

'I brought you here for a demonstration.'

The commander leaned over the open container. Inside, in snug foam packing, were a flat vacuum-packed package and a triple-band VHF transmitter. Resting on top was Holly's locator. Root groaned. Holly wouldn't willingly give up her equipment; no LEP officer would.

'What sort of demonstration, you demented freak?'

Again that cold chuckle.

'A demonstration of my utter commitment to my goals.'

Root should have started to worry about his own health then, but he was too busy worrying about Holly's.

'If you've harmed one tip of my officer's pointy ears ...'

'*Your* officer? Oh, we have management. How privileged. All the better to make my point.'

Alarm bells went off in Root's head.

'Your point?'

The voice emanating from the aluminium speaker grid was as serious as nuclear winter.

'My point, little fairy man, is that I am not someone to be trifled with. Now, if you would please observe the package.'

The commander duly observed. It was a nondescript enough shape. Flat, like a slab of putty, or … Oh no.

Beneath the sealant, a red light flicked on.

'Fly, little fairy,' said the voice. 'And tell your friends Artemis Fowl the Second says hello.'

Beside the red light, green symbols began to click through a routine. Root recognized them from his human studies class back in the Academy. They were … numbers. Going backwards. A countdown!

'D'Arvit!' growled Root. (There is no point translating that word as it would have to be censored.)

He turned and fled up the corridor, Artemis Fowl's mocking tones carrying down the metal funnel.

'Three,' said the human. 'Two …'

'D'Arvit,' repeated Root.

The corridor seemed much longer now. A sliver of starry sky peeked through a wedge of open door. Root activated his wings. This would take some fancy flying. The Hummingbird's span was barely narrower than the ship's corridor.

'One.'

Sparks flew as the electronic wings scraped a protruding pipe. Root cartwheeled, righting himself at MACH 1.

'Zero …' said the voice. 'Boom!'

Inside the vacuum-packed package, a detonator sparked, igniting a kilogram of pure Semtex. The white-hot reaction devoured the surrounding oxygen in a nanosecond and surged down the path of least resistance, which was, of course, immediately after LEP Commander Root.

Root dropped his visor, opening the throttle to maximum. The door was metres away now. It was just a matter of what reached it first – the fairy or the fireball.

He made it. Barely. He could feel the explosion rattling his torso as he threw himself into a reverse loop. Flames latched on to his jumpsuit, licking along his legs. Root continued his manoeuvre, crashing directly into the icy water. He broke the surface swearing.

Above him, the whaler had been totally consumed by noxious flames.

'Commander,' came a voice in his earpiece. It was Foaly. He was back in range.

'Commander. What's your status?'

Root lifted free of the water's grip.

'My status, Foaly, is extremely annoyed. Get on your computers. I want to know everything there is to know about one Artemis Fowl, and I want to know it before I get back to base.'

'Yessir, Commander. Right away.'

No wisecrack. Even Foaly realized that this was not the time.

Root hovered at 300 metres. Below him the blazing

CHAPTER 6: SÏEGE

 ARTEMÏS leaned back in the study's leather swivel chair, smiling over steepled fingers. Perfect. That little explosion should cure those fairies of their cavalier attitude. Plus there was one less whaler in the world. Artemis Fowl did not like whalers. There were less objectionable ways to produce oil by-products.

The pinhole camera concealed in the locator had worked perfectly. With its high-resolution images he had picked out the fairy's tell-tale breath crystals.

Artemis consulted the basement surveillance monitor. His captive was sitting on the cot now, head in hands. Artemis frowned. He hadn't expected the fairy to appear so … human. Until now, they had merely been quarry. Animals to be hunted. But now, seeing one like this, in obvious discomfort, it changed things.

Artemis put the computer to sleep and crossed to the main doors. Time for a little chat with their guest. Just as his fingers alighted on the brass handles, the door flew open before him. Juliet appeared in the doorway, cheeks flushed from haste.

'Artemis,' she gasped. 'Your mother. She ...'

Artemis felt a lead ball drop in his stomach.

'Yes?'

'Well, she says, Artemis ... Artemis, that your ...'

'Yes, Juliet. For heaven's sake, what is it?'

Juliet placed both hands over her mouth, composing herself. After several seconds she parted spangled nails, speaking through her fingers.

'It's your father, sir. Artemis Senior. Madam Fowl says he's come back!'

For a split second, Artemis could have sworn his heart had stopped. Father? Back? Was it possible? Of course he'd always believed his father was alive. But lately, since he'd hatched this fairy scheme, it was almost as if his father had shifted to the back of his mind. Artemis felt guilt churn his stomach. He had given up. Given up on his own father.

'Did you see him, Juliet? With your own eyes?'

The girl shook her head.

'No, Artemis, sir. I just heard voices. In the bedroom. But she won't let me through the door. Not for anything. Not even with a hot drink.'

Artemis calculated. They had returned barely an hour since. His father could have slipped past Juliet. It was possible. Just possible. He glanced at his watch, synchronized with Greenwich Mean Time by constantly updated radio signals. Three a.m. Time was ticking on. His entire plan depended on the fairies making their next move before daylight.

Artemis started. He was doing it again, pushing family to one side. What was he becoming? His father was the priority here, not some money-making scheme.

Juliet was still in the doorway, watching him with those enormous blue eyes. She was waiting for him to make a decision, as he always did. And for once, there was indecision scrawled across his pale features.

'Very well,' he mumbled eventually. 'I had better go up there immediately.'

Artemis brushed past the girl, taking the steps two at a time. His mother's room was two flights up, a converted attic space.

He hesitated at the door. What would he say if it was his father miraculously returned? What would he do? It was ridiculous dithering about it. Impossible to predict. He knocked lightly.

'Mother?'

No response, but he thought he heard a giggle and was instantly transported into the past. Initially this room had been his parents' lounge. They would sit on the chaise longue for hours, tittering like school children, feeding the pigeons or watching the ships sailing past on Dublin

sound. When Artemis Senior had disappeared, Angeline Fowl had become more and more attached to the space, eventually refusing to leave altogether.

'Mother? Are you all right?'

Muffled voices from within. Conspiratorial whispers.

'Mother. I'm coming in.'

'Wait a moment. Timmy, stop it, you beast. We have company.'

Timmy? Artemis's heart thumped like a snare drum in his chest. Timmy, her pet name for his father. Timmy and Arty. The two men in her life. He could wait no longer. Artemis burst through the double doors.

His first impression was light. Mother had the lamps on. A good sign surely. Artemis knew where his mother would be. He knew exactly where to look. But he couldn't. What if … What if …

'Yes, can we help you?'

Artemis turned, his eyes still downcast. 'It's me.'

His mother laughed. Airy and carefree. 'I can see it's you, Papa. Can't you even give your boy one night off? It is our honeymoon after all.'

Artemis knew then. It was just an escalation of her madness. Papa? Angeline thought Artemis was his own grandfather. Dead over ten years. He raised his gaze slowly.

His mother was seated on the chaise longue, resplendent in her own wedding dress, face clumsily coated with make-up. But that wasn't the worst of it.

Beside her was a facsimile of his father, constructed from the morning suit he'd worn on that glorious day in Christchurch Cathedral fourteen years ago. The clothes were padded with tissue, and atop the dress shirt was a stuffed pillowcase with lipstick features. It was almost funny. Artemis choked back a sob, his hopes vanishing like a summer rainbow.

'What do you say, Papa?' said Angeline in a deep bass, nodding the pillow like a ventriloquist manipulating her dummy. 'One night off for your boy, eh?'

Artemis nodded. What else could he do?

'One night then. Take tomorrow too. Be happy.'

Angeline's face radiated honest joy. She sprang from the couch, embracing her unrecognized son.

'Thank you, Papa. Thank you.'

Artemis returned the embrace, though it felt like cheating.

'You're welcome, Mo— Angeline. Now, I must be off. Business to attend to.'

His mother settled beside her imitation husband.

'Yes, Papa. You go, don't worry, we can keep ourselves amused.'

Artemis left. He didn't look back. There were things to be done. Fairies to be extorted. He had no time for his mother's fantasy world.

*

Captain Holly Short was holding her head in her hands. One hand to be precise. The other was scrabbling down the side of her boot, on the camera's blindside. In actuality her head was crystal clear, but it would do no harm for the enemy to believe her still out of action. Perhaps they would underestimate her. And that would be the last mistake they ever made.

Holly's fingers closed around the object that had been digging into her ankle. She knew immediately by its contours what was concealed there. The acorn! It must have slipped into her boot during all the commotion by the oak. This could be a vital development. All she needed was a small patch of earth, then her powers would be restored.

Holly glanced surreptitiously around the cell. Fresh concrete by the looks of it. Not a single crack or flaky corner. Nowhere to bury her secret weapon. Holly stood tentatively, trying out her legs for stability. Not too bad, a bit shaky around the knees, but otherwise sound enough. She crossed to the wall, pressing her cheek and palms to the smooth surface. The concrete was fresh all right, very recent. Still damp in patches. Obviously her prison had been specially prepared.

'Looking for something?' said a voice. A cold, heartless voice.

Holly reared back from the wall. The human boy was standing not two metres from her, his eyes hidden behind mirrored glasses. He had entered the room without a sound. Extraordinary.

'Sit, please.'

Holly did not want to sit please. What she wanted to do was incapacitate this insolent pup with her elbow and use his miserable hide for leverage. Artemis could see it in her eyes. It amused him.

'Getting ideas, are we, Captain Short?'

Holly bared her teeth, it was answer enough.

'We are both fully aware of the rules here, Captain. This is my house. You must abide by my wishes. Your laws, not mine. Obviously my wishes do not include bodily harm to myself, or you attempting to leave this house.'

It hit Holly then.

'How do you know my –'

'Your name? Your rank?' Artemis smiled, though there was no joy in it. 'If you will wear a name tag ...'

Holly's hand unconsciously covered the silver tag on her suit.

'But that's written in –'

'Gnommish. I know. I happen to be fluent. As is everyone in my network.'

Holly was silent for a moment, processing this momentous revelation.

'Fowl,' she said with feeling, 'you have no idea what you've done. Bringing the worlds together like this could mean disaster for us all.'

120

Artemis shrugged. 'I am not concerned with *us all*, just myself. And believe me, I shall be perfectly fine. Now, sit, please.'

Holly sat, never taking her hazel eyes from the diminutive monster before her.

'So what is this master plan, Fowl? Let me guess: world domination?'

'Nothing so melodramatic,' chuckled Artemis. 'Just riches.'

'A thief!' spat Holly. 'You're just a thief!'

Annoyance flashed across Artemis's features, only to be replaced by his customary sardonic grin.

'Yes. A thief if you like. Hardly *just* a thief though. The world's first cross-species thief.'

Captain Short snorted. 'First cross-species thief! Mud People have been stealing from us for millennia. Why do you think we live underground?'

'True. But I will be first to successfully separate a fairy from its gold.'

'Gold? Gold? Human idiot. You don't honestly believe that crock-of-gold nonsense. Some things aren't true, you know.'

Holly threw her head back and laughed.

Artemis checked his nails patiently, waiting for her to finish. When the gales had finally subsided, he shook his index finger.

'You are right to laugh, Captain Short. For a while

there, I did believe in all that under-the-rainbow crock-of-gold blarney, but now I know better. Now I know about the hostage fund.'

Holly struggled to keep her face under control.

'What hostage fund?'

'Oh, come now, Captain. Why bother with the charade? You told me about it yourself.'

'I-I told you!' stammered Holly. 'Ridiculous!'

'Look at your arm.'

Holly rolled up her right sleeve. There was a small cotton pad taped to the vein.

'That's where we administered the sodium pentathol. Commonly known as truth serum. You sang like a bird.'

Holly knew it was true. How else could he know?

'You're mad!'

Artemis nodded indulgently. 'If I win, I'm a prodigy. If I lose then I'm mad. That's the way history is written.'

Of course, there had been no sodium pentathol, just a harmless prick with a sterilized needle. Artemis would not risk causing brain damage to his meal ticket, but nor could he afford to reveal the Book as the source of his information. Better to let the hostage believe that she had betrayed her own people. It would lower her morale, making her more susceptible to his mind games. Still, the ruse disturbed him. It was undeniably cruel. How far was he prepared to go for this gold? He didn't know, and wouldn't until the time came.

Holly slumped, momentarily defeated by this latest development. She had talked. Revealed sacred secrets. Even if she did manage to escape, she would be banished to some freezing tunnel under the Arctic Circle.

'This isn't over, Fowl,' she said at last. 'We have powers you can't possibly know about. It would take days to describe them all.'

The infuriating boy laughed again. 'How long do you think you've been here?'

Holly groaned; she knew what was coming. 'A few hours?'

Artemis shook his head. 'Three days,' he lied. 'We've had you on a drip for over sixty hours ... until you told us everything we needed to know.'

Even as the words came out, Artemis felt guilty. These mind games were having an obvious effect on Holly, destroying her from the inside out. Was there really a need for this?

'Three days? You could have killed me. What kind of ...'

And it was that speechless quality that sent the doubt shooting through Artemis's brain. The fairy thought him so evil, she couldn't even find the words.

Holly pulled herself together.

'Well then, Master Fowl,' she spat, heavy on the contempt, 'if you know so much about us, then you know what happens when they locate me.'

Artemis nodded absently. 'Oh yes, I know. In fact, I'm counting on it.'

It was Holly's turn to grin.

'Oh really. Tell me, boy, have you ever met a troll?'

For the first time, the human's confidence dropped a notch.

'No. Never a troll.'

Holly showed more teeth.

'You will, Fowl. You will. And I hope I'm there to see it.'

The LEP had established a surface Op's HQ at E1: Tara.

'Well?' said Root, slapping at a paramedic gremlin who was applying burn salve to his forehead. 'Leave it. The magic will sort me out soon enough.'

'Well what?' replied Foaly.

'Don't give me any of your lip today, Foaly, because today is not one of those Oh-I'm-so-impressed-with-the-pony's-technology days. Tell me what you found on the human.'

Foaly scowled, securing his foil hat on his head. He flipped the top on a wafer-thin laptop.

'I hacked into Interpol. Not too difficult, I can tell you. They might as well have put out a welcome mat ...'

Root drummed his fingers on the conference table. 'Get on with it.'

'Right. Fowl. Ten-gigabyte file. In paper terms that's half a library.'

The commander whistled. 'That's one busy human.'

'Family,' corrected Foaly. 'The Fowls have been subverting justice for generations. Racketeering, smuggling, armed robbery. Mostly corporate crime last century.'

'So do we have a location?'

'That was the easy bit. Fowl Manor. On a two-hundred-acre estate on the outskirts of Dublin. Fowl Manor is only about twenty klicks from our current location.'

Root chewed his bottom lip.

'Only twenty? That means we could make it before first light.'

'Yep. Sort out this whole mess before it gets out of hand in the rays of the sun.'

The commander nodded. This was their first break. Fairies had not operated in natural light for centuries. Even when they had lived above ground, they were essentially night creatures. The sun diluted their magic like bleaching a photograph. If they had to wait another day before sending in a strike force, who knew what damage Fowl could achieve?

It was even possible that this whole affair was media-oriented, and by tomorrow evening Captain Short's face would be on the cover of every publication on the planet.

Root shuddered. That would spell the end of everything, unless the Mud People had learned to coexist with other species. And if history had taught him any lessons it was that humans couldn't get along with anyone, even themselves.

'Right. Everyone, lock and load. V flight pattern. Establish a perimeter inside the Manor grounds.'

The Retrieval Squad roared military-type affirmatives, coaxing as many metallic noises from their weapons as possible.

'Foaly, round up the techies. Follow us in the shuttle. And bring the big dishes. We'll shut down the entire estate, give ourselves a bit of breathing room.'

'One thing, Commander,' mused Foaly.

'Yes?' said Root impatiently.

'Why did this human tell us who he was? He must have known we could find him.'

Root shrugged. 'Maybe he's not as clever as he thinks he is.'

'No. I don't think that's it. I don't think that's it at all. I think he's been one step ahead of us all the way, and this is no different.'

'I don't have time for theorizing now, Foaly. First light is approaching.'

'One more thing, Commander.'

'Is this important?'

'Yes, I think it is.'

'Well?'

Foaly tapped a key on his laptop, scrolling through Artemis's vital statistics.

'This criminal mastermind, the one behind this elaborate scheme …'

'Yes? What about him?'

Foaly looked up, an almost admiring look in his golden eyes.

'Well, he's only twelve years old. And that's young, even for a human.'

Root snorted, jacking a new battery into his tri-barrelled blaster.

'Too much damned TV. Thinks he's Sherlock Holmes.'

'That's Professor Moriarty,' corrected Foaly.

'Holmes, Moriarty, they both look the same with the flesh scorched off their skulls.'

And with that elegant parting riposte, Root followed his squad into the night air.

The Retrieval Squad adopted the V goose formation with Root on point. They flew south-west, following the video feed e-mailed to their helmets. Foaly had even marked Fowl Manor with a red dot. Idiot-proof, he'd muttered into his mouthpiece, just loud enough for the commander to hear him.

The centrepiece of the Fowl estate was a renovated late-medieval/early-modern castle, built by Lord Hugh Fowl in the fifteenth century.

The Fowls had held on to Fowl Manor over the years, surviving war, civil unrest and several tax audits. Artemis did not intend to be the one to lose it.

The estate was ringed by a five-metre crenellated stone wall, complete with the original guard towers and walkways. The Retrieval Squad put down just inside the boundary and began an immediate scan for possible hostiles.

'Twenty metres apart,' instructed Root. 'Sweep the area. Check in every sixty seconds. Clear?'

Retrieval nodded. Of course it was clear. They were professionals.

Lieutenant Cudgeon, Retrieval Squad's leader, climbed a guard tower.

'You know what we should do, Julius?'

He and Root had been in the Academy together, brought up in the same tunnel. Cudgeon was one of perhaps five fairies who called Root by his first name.

'I know what you think we should do.'

'We should blast the whole place.'

'What a surprise.'

'The cleanest way. One blue rinse and our losses are minimum.'

Blue rinse was the slang term for the devastating biological bomb used on rare occasions by the force. The clever thing about a bio-bomb was that it destroyed only living tissue. The landscape was unchanged.

)꒒)ꗋꗆꗆꗋ•ꗋ•꒒)II꒒ꗆꗋ•ꕥ•

'That minimum loss you're talking about happens to be one of my officers.'

'Oh yes,' tutted Cudgeon. 'A female Recon officer. The test case. Well, I don't think you'll have any problem justifying a tactical solution.'

Root's face took on that familiar purple hue.

'The best thing you can do right now is stay out of my way, or else I may be forced to ram that blue rinse straight into that morass you call a brain.'

Cudgeon was unperturbed. 'Insulting me doesn't change the facts, Julius. You know what the Book says. We cannot under any circumstances allow the Lower Elements to be compromised. One time-stop is all you get, after that ...'

The lieutenant didn't finish his statement. He didn't have to.

'I know what the Book says,' snapped Root. 'I just wish you weren't so gung-ho about it. If I didn't know you better, I'd say there was some human blood in you.'

'There's no call for that,' pouted Cudgeon. 'I'm only doing my job.'

'Point taken,' conceded the commander. 'I'm sorry.'

You didn't often hear Root apologizing, but then it had been a deeply offensive insult.

Butler was on monitors.

'Anything?' asked Artemis.

Butler started; he hadn't heard the young master come in.

'No. Nothing. Once or twice I thought I saw a flicker, but it turned out to be nothing.'

'Nothing is nothing,' commented Artemis cryptically. 'Use the new camera.'

Butler nodded. Only last month, Master Fowl had purchased a cine-camera over the Internet. Two thousand frames a second, recently developed by Industrial Light and Magic for specialized nature shoots, hummingbird wings and such. It processed images faster than the human eye could. Artemis had had it installed behind a cherub over the main entrance.

Butler activated the joypad.

'Where?'

'Try the avenue. I have a feeling visitors are on the way.'

The manservant manipulated the toothpick-sized stick with his massive fingers. A live image sprang into life on the digital monitor.

'Nothing,' muttered Butler. 'Quiet as the grave.'

Artemis pointed to the control desk.

'Freeze it.'

Butler nearly queried the order. Nearly. Instead he held his tongue and pressed the pad. On screen, the cherry trees froze, blossoms trapped in mid-air. More importantly, a dozen or so black-clad figures suddenly appeared on the avenue.

'What!' exclaimed Butler. 'Where did they spring from?'

'They're shielded,' explained Artemis. 'Vibrating at high speed. Too fast for the human eye to follow ...'

'But not for the camera,' nodded Butler. Master Artemis. Always two steps ahead. 'If only I could carry it around with me.'

'If only. But we do have the next best thing ...'

Artemis lifted a headset gingerly from the workbench. It was the remains of Holly's helmet. Obviously, trying to cram Butler's head into the original helmet would be like trying to fit a potato into a thimble. Only the visor and control buttons were intact. Straps from a hard hat had been jury-rigged to fit the manservant's cranium.

'This thing is equipped with several filters. It stands to reason that one of them is anti-shield. Let's try it out, shall we?'

Artemis placed the set over Butler's ears.

'Obviously with your eye span, there are going to be blind spots, but that shouldn't hamper you unduly. Now, run the camera.'

Butler set the camera rolling again, while Artemis slotted down one filter after another.

'Now?'

'No.'

'Now ...'

'Everything's gone red. Ultraviolet. No fairies.'

'Now?'

'No. Polaroid, I think.'

'Last one.'

Butler smiled. A shark that's spotted a bare behind.

'Gottem.'

Butler was seeing the world as it was, complete with LEPretrieval team sweeping the avenue.

'Hmm,' said Artemis. 'Strobe variation, I would guess. Very high frequency.'

'I see,' fibbed Butler.

'Metaphorically or literally?' smiled his employer.

'Exactly.'

Artemis shook himself. More jokes. Next thing he'd be wearing clown shoes and turning cartwheels in the main hall.

'Very well, Butler. Time for you to do what you do best. We appear to have intruders in the grounds ...'

Butler stood. No further instructions were necessary. He tightened the hard-hat straps, striding brusquely to the door.

'Oh, and Butler.'

'Yes, Artemis?'

'I prefer scared to dead. If possible.'

Butler nodded. If possible.

LEPretrieval One were the best and the brightest. It was every little fairy's dream that one day he would grow up to don the stealth-black jumpsuit of the Retrieval commandos. These were the elite. Trouble was their middle name. In the case of Captain Kelp, Trouble was actually his first name. He'd insisted on it at his manhood ceremony, having just been accepted into the Academy.

Trouble led his team down the sweeping avenue. As usual, he took the point position himself, determined to be the first into the fray if, as he fervently hoped, a fray developed.

'Check in,' he whispered into the mike that wound snake-like from his helmet.

'Negative on one.'

'Nothing, Captain.'

'A big negatori, Trouble.'

Captain Kelp winced.

'We're in the field, Corporal. Follow procedure.'

'But Mummy said!'

'I don't care what Mummy said, Corporal! Rank is rank! You will refer to me as Captain Kelp.'

'Yessir, Captain,' sulked the corporal. 'But don't ask me to iron your tunic any more.'

Trouble zeroed in on his brother's channel, shutting out the rest of the squad.

'Shut up about Mummy, will you? And the ironing. You're only on this mission because I requested you! Now start acting like a professional or get back to the perimeter!'

'OK, Trubs.'

'Trouble!' shouted Captain Kelp. 'It's Trouble. Not Trubs, or Trub. Trouble! OK?'

'OK. *Trouble*. Mummy's right. You're only a baby.'

Swearing very unprofessionally, Captain Kelp switched his headset back to the open channel. He was just in time to hear an unusual sound.

'*Arrkk.*'

'What was that?'

'What?'

'Dunno.'

'Nothing, Captain.'

But Trouble had done a Sound Recognition in-service for his captain's exam, and he was pretty sure the '*Arrkk*' had been caused by someone getting a chop across the windpipe. More than likely his brother had walked into a shrub.

'Grub? Are you all right?'

'That's Corporal Grub to you.'

Kelp viciously kicked a daisy.

'Check in. Sound off in sequence.'

'One, OK.'

'Two, fine.'

'Three, bored but alive.'

'Five approaching west wing.'

Kelp froze. 'Wait. Four? You there, Four? What's your situation?'

'.................' Nothing except static.

'Right. Four is down. Possibly an equipment malfunction. Still, we can't afford to take any chances. Regroup by the main door.'

Retrieval One crept together, making slightly less noise than a silk spider. Kelp did a quick head count. Eleven. One short of a full complement. Four was probably wandering around the rose bushes, wondering why nobody was talking to him.

Then Trouble noticed two things – one, a pair of black boots was sticking out of a shrub beside the door, and two, there was a massive human standing in the doorway. The figure was cradling a very nasty-looking gun in the crook of his arm.

'Go silent,' whispered Kelp, and immediately eleven full-face visors slid down to seal in the sounds of his squad's breathing and communications.

'Now, nobody panic. I think I can trace the sequence of events here. Four is skulking around outside the door. The Mud Man opens it. Four gets a whack on the noggin and lands in the bushes. No problem. Our cover is intact. Repeat intact. So no itchy fingers, please. Grub ... Sorry, Corporal Kelp, check Four's vitals. The rest of you make a hole and keep it quiet.'

The squad stepped back carefully until they were standing on the manicured grassy verge. The figure before them was indeed impressive, without doubt the biggest human any of them had ever seen.

'D'Arvit,' breathed Two.

'Maintain radio silence, except in emergencies,' ordered Kelp. 'Swearing is hardly an emergency.' Secretly, however, he concurred with the sentiment. This was one time he was glad to be shielded. That man looked as if he could squash half a dozen fairies in one massive fist.

Grub returned to his slot. 'Four is stable. Concussed, I'd guess. But otherwise OK. His shield's off though, so I stuffed him in the bushes.'

'Well done, Corporal. Good thinking.'

The last thing they needed was for Four's boots to be spotted.

The man moved, lumbering casually along the path. He may have glanced left or right, it was difficult to tell beneath the hood pulled over his eyes. Odd for a human to wear a hood on such a fine night.

'Safety catches off,' ordered Trouble.

He imagined his men rolling their eyes. Like they hadn't had their safeties off for the last half an hour. Still, you had to go by the book, in case of a tribunal later on. There was a time when Retrieval blasted first and answered questions never. But not any more. Now there was always some do-gooder civilian banging on about civil rights. Even for humans, would you believe it?

The man mountain stopped, right in the middle of the squad. If he had been able to see them, it would be the perfect tactical position. Their own firearms were virtually useless, as they would probably do more damage to each other than the human.

Fortunately the entire squad was invisible, with the exception of Four, who was safely secreted in what appeared to be a rhododendron.

'Buzz batons. Fire 'em up.'

Just in case. No harm in being cautious.

And when the LEP officers were switching weapons, right at that moment when their hands were fumbling with holsters, that's when the Mud Man spoke.

'Evening, gentlemen,' he said, sweeping back his hood.

Funny that, thought Trouble. It was almost as if … Then he saw the makeshift goggles.

'Cover!' he screamed. 'Cover!'

But it was too late. No option but to stand and fight. And that was no option at all.

Butler could have taken them from the parapet. One at a time with the ivory hunter's rifle. But that wasn't the plan. This was all about making an impression. Sending a message. It was standard procedure with any police force in the world to send in the cannon fodder first before opening negotiations. It was almost expected that they would meet with resistance, and Butler was happy to oblige.

He peeked out through the letter box and, oh

happy coincidence, there was a pair of goggled eyes peeking right back at him. It was just too fortuitous to pass up.

'Bed time,' said Butler, heaving the door with a mighty shoulder. The fairy flew several metres before alighting in the shrubbery. Juliet would be devastated. She loved rhododendrons. One down. Several to go.

Butler pulled up the peaked hood on his field jacket, stepping into the porch. There they were, spread out like a squadron of Action Men. If not for the array of very proficient-looking weaponry hanging from each belt, it would have been almost comical.

Sliding his finger casually under the trigger guard, Butler strode into their midst. The bulky one at two o'clock was giving the orders. You could tell from the heads angled his way.

The leader gave a command and the squad switched to close-quarters weapons. It made sense, they'd only cut themselves to pieces with firearms. Time for action.

'Evening, gentlemen,' Butler said. He couldn't help it, and it was worth it for that one moment of consternation. Then his gun was up and blazing.

Captain Kelp was the first casualty, a titanium-tipped dart puncturing the neck of his suit. He went down sluggishly, as though the air had turned to water. Two more of the squad were dropped before they had any idea what was going on.

It must be quite traumatic, thought Butler dispassionately, to lose an advantage that you've held for centuries.

By now, the remains of Retrieval One had their buzz batons fired up and raised. But they made the mistake of hanging back, waiting for a command that was not forthcoming. This gave Butler an opportunity to take the fight to them. As if he needed another advantage.

Even so, for a second the manservant hesitated. These beings were so small. Like children. Then Grub clipped him on the elbow with his buzz baton and 1,000 volts spread across Butler's chest. All sympathy for the little people vanished instantly.

Butler grabbed the offending baton, swinging weapon and bearer like a set of bolas. Grub squealed as he was released, his new-found momentum carrying him directly into three of his comrades.

Butler continued the swinging motion, driving punishing punches into the chests of two more fairies. Another clambered on to his back, stinging him repeatedly with the baton. Butler fell on him. Something cracked and the stinging stopped.

Suddenly there was a barrel under his chin. One of Retrieval had managed to get his weapon cocked.

'Freeze, Mud Boy,' droned a helmet-filtered voice. It was a serious-looking gun, liquid coolant bubbled along its length. 'Just give me a reason.'

Butler rolled his eyes. Different race, same macho clichés. He slapped the fairy open-handed. To the little man it must have been like the sky falling on his head.

'That reason enough for you?'

Butler scrambled to his feet. Fairy bodies were scattered around him in various stages of shock and unconsciousness. Scared definitely. Dead, probably not. Mission accomplished.

One little chap was faking though. You could tell by the way his tiny knees knocked together. Butler picked him up by the neck, finger and thumb easily meeting around the back.

'Name?'

'G-Grub ... er, I mean Corporal Kelp.'

'Well, Corporal, you tell your commander that the next time I see armed forces coming in here, they'll be picked off by sniper fire. No darts either. Armour-piercing bullets.'

'Yessir. Sniper fire. Got it. Seems fair.'

'Good. You are, however, permitted to remove your injured.'

'Most generous of you.'

'But if I see so much as the twinkle of a weapon on any of the medics, I might be tempted to detonate a few of the mines I have planted in the grounds.'

Grub swallowed, his pallor increasing behind the visor.

'Unarmed medics. Crystal clear.'

Butler set the fairy down, brushing his tunic with massive fingers.

'Now. Final thing. Listening?'

Furious nods.

'I want a negotiator. Someone who can make decisions. Not some no-ranker who has to run off back to base after every demand. Understood?'

'Fine. That is, I'm sure it will be fine. Unfortunately I'm one of those no-rankers. So, you see, I can't actually guarantee it will be fine ...'

Butler was sorely tempted to drop-kick this little fellow back to his camp.

'Very well. I understand. Just ... shut up!'

Grub almost agreed, then he clamped his mouth shut and nodded.

'Good. Now, before you go, collect all weapons and helmets and make a little pile right there.'

Grub took a deep breath. Ah well, may as well go out a hero.

'I can't do that.'

'Oh, really? And why not?'

Grub drew himself up to his full height. 'An LEP officer never relinquishes his weapon.'

Butler nodded. 'Fair enough. Thought I'd ask. Off you go then.'

Hardly able to believe his luck, Grub scurried back towards the command tower. He was the last fairy standing. Trouble was snoring in the gravel but he, Grub Kelp, had faced down the Mud Monster. Wait until Mummy heard about this.

Holly sat on the edge of her bed, fingers curled around the metal base. She lifted slowly, taking the weight on her arms. The strain threatened to pop her elbows from their sockets. She held it for a second, and then slammed the frame into the concrete. A satisfying cloud of dust and splinters swirled around her knees.

'Good,' she grunted.

Holly eyed the camera. Doubtless they were watching her. No time to waste. She flexed her fingers, repeating the manoeuvre again and again, until the steel base left deep weals in her finger joints. With each impact more and more splinters popped from the fresh floor.

After several moments, the cell door burst open and Juliet fell into the room.

'What are you doing?' she panted. 'Trying to knock the house down?'

'I'm hungry!' shouted Holly. 'And I'm fed up waving at that stupid camera. Don't you feed your prisoners around here? I want some food!'

Juliet's fingers curled into a fist. Artemis had warned her to be civil, but there was a limit.

'No need to get your knick … or whatever in a twist. So what do you fairies eat?'

'Got any dolphin?' Holly asked sarcastically.

Juliet shuddered. 'No, I don't, you beast!'

'Fruit then. Or vegetables. Make sure they're washed. I don't want any of your chemical poisons in my blood.'

'Ha ha, you're a riot, you are. Don't worry, all our produce is grown naturally.' Juliet paused on her way to the door. 'And don't you go forgetting the rules. No trying to escape from the house. And there's no need to break up the furniture either. Don't make me demonstrate my full nelson.'

As soon as Juliet's footsteps had faded, Holly began smashing the bed into the concrete. That was the thing about fairy bonds. The instructions had to be given eye to eye, and they had to be very precise. Just saying there was no need to do a thing wasn't specifically forbidding an elf to do it. And another thing, Holly had no intention of escaping from the house. That wasn't to say that she didn't mean to get out of her cell.

Artemis had added yet another monitor to the bank. This one was linked to a camera in Angeline Fowl's attic room. He spared a moment to check on his mother. Sometimes it bothered him having a camera in her room; it seemed almost like spying. But it was for her own good. There was always the danger that she could hurt herself. At the moment she was sleeping peacefully, having swallowed the sleeping pill that Juliet had left on her tray. All part of the plan. A vital part, as it happened.

Butler entered the control room. He was clutching a fistful of fairy hardware and rubbing his neck.

'Tricky little blighters.'

Artemis looked up from the monitor bank.

'Any problems?'

'Nothing major. These little batons pack quite a punch though. How's our prisoner?'

'Fine. Juliet is getting her something to eat. I'm afraid Captain Short is going a bit stir-crazy.'

On the screen, Holly was smashing her cot into the concrete.

'It's understandable,' noted the manservant. 'Imagine her frustration. It's not as if she can tunnel her way out.'

Artemis smiled. 'No. The entire estate is built on a bed of limestone. Not even a dwarf could tunnel his way out of here. Or in.'

Wrong, as it happened. Dead wrong. A landmark moment for Artemis Fowl.

The LEP had procedures for emergencies like this one. Admittedly these did not include the Retrieval Squad getting hammered by a lone enemy. Still, that just made the next step all the more urgent, especially with the faintest of orange tinges creeping into the sky.

'Are we good to go?' roared Root into his mike, as though it wasn't whisper-sensitive.

⊞ ⚮ • ◉ ◊ ⚭ ⯅ ⚮ • ⵀ ◉ ⚮ • ⌘ ⦵ ⚮ ⯈ • ◌ • ⚮ ⵕ

Good to go, thought Foaly, busy wiring the last dish on
a watchtower. These military types and their catchphrases.
Good to go, lock and load, I don't know but I've been
told. So insecure.

Aloud he said, 'No need to shout, Commander. These
headsets could pick up a spider scratching in Madagascar.'

'And is there a spider scratching in Madagascar?'

'Well ... I don't know. They can't really –'

'Well, stop changing the subject, Foaly, and answer the
question!'

The centaur scowled. The commander took everything
so literally. He plugged the dish's modem lead into his
laptop.

'OK. We're ... good to go.'

'About time too. Right, flip the switch.'

For the third time in as many moments, Foaly gritted
his horsy teeth. He was indeed the stereotypical
unappreciated genius. Flick the switch, if you don't mind.
Root didn't have the cranial capacity to appreciate what
he was trying to do here.

Stopping time wasn't just a matter of pressing the *on*
button: there was a series of delicate procedures that had
to be performed with utmost precision. Otherwise the
stop zone could end up as just so much ash and radioactive
slop.

While it was true that fairies had been stopping time
for millennia, these days, with satellite communication

and the Internet, humans were liable to notice if a zone just dropped out of time for a couple of hours. There was an age when you could throw a blanket stoppage over a whole country and the Mud People would simply think the gods were angry. But not any more. Nowadays the humans had instruments for measuring anything, so if there was any time-stopping to be done, it had better be fine-tuned and precise.

In the old days, five elfin warlocks would form a pentagram around the target and spread a magic shield over it, temporarily stopping time inside the enchanted enclosure.

This was fine as far as it went, provided the warlocks didn't have to use the bathroom. Many a siege was lost because an elf had one glass of wine too many. Warlocks tire quickly too, and their arms get sore. On a good day, you had maybe an hour and a half, which was hardly worth the trouble in the first place.

It was Foaly's idea to mechanize the whole procedure. He had the warlocks do their thing into lithium batteries, and then he set up a network of receiver dishes around the designated area. Sounds simple? Well, it wasn't. But there were definite advantages. For one thing there were no more power surges. Batteries didn't try to show off to each other. You could calculate exactly how many power cells were needed, and sieges could be extended for up to eight hours.

As it happened, the Fowl estate was the perfect location for a time-stop – isolated with a definite boundary. It even had elevated towers for the dishes, for heaven's sake. It was almost as if Artemis Fowl wanted time stopped … Foaly's finger hesitated over the button. Could it be possible? After all, the human youth had been one step ahead throughout this whole affair.

'Commander?'

'Are we on-line yet?'

'Not exactly. There's something –'

Root's reaction nearly blew out the woofers in Foaly's earpiece.

'No, Foaly! There isn't something! None of your bright ideas, thank you very much. Captain Short's life is in danger, so push the button before I climb that tower and push it with your face!'

'Touchy,' muttered Foaly, and pushed the button.

Lieutenant Cudgeon checked his moonometer.

'You have eight hours.'

'I know how much time I have,' growled Root. 'And stop following me. Don't you have work to do?'

'Actually, now that you mention it, I have a bio-bomb to arm.'

Root rounded on him. 'Don't annoy me, Lieutenant. Having you pass comments at every turn is not improving my concentration. Just do whatever it is you feel you have to do. But be prepared to back it up at tribunal. If this one goes wrong, heads are going to roll.'

'Indeed,' muttered Cudgeon under his breath. 'But mine is not going to be one of them.'

Root checked the sky. A shimmering azure field had descended over the Fowl estate. Good. They were in limbo. Outside the walls, life continued at an exaggerated pace, but if anyone were to somehow gain access to the manor in spite of the fortified walls and high gate, they would find it deserted, all occupants trapped in the past.

So for the next eight hours, it would be twilight on the Fowl estate. After that, Root could not guarantee Holly's safety. Given the gravity of the situation, it was more than likely that Cudgeon would get the go-ahead to bio-bomb the whole place. Root had seen a blue rinse before. No living thing escaped, not even the rats.

Root caught up with Foaly at the base of the north tower. The centaur had parked a shuttle by the metre-thick wall. Already the work area was a mess of tangled wires and pulsating fibre optics.

'Foaly? Are you in here?'

The centaur's foil-capped head emerged from the belly of a disembowelled hard drive.

'Over here, Commander. You've come to push a button with my face, I presume.'

Root almost laughed. 'Don't tell me you're looking for

an apology, Foaly. I've already used my quota for today. And that was to a lifelong friend.'

'Cudgeon? Forgive me, Commander, but I wouldn't waste my apologies on the lieutenant. He won't be wasting any on you when he stabs you in the back.'

'You're wrong about him. Cudgeon is a good officer. A bit eager, certainly, but he'll do the right thing when the time comes.'

'The right thing for himself maybe. I don't think Holly is at the top of his priority list.'

Root didn't answer. He couldn't.

'And another thing. I have a sneaking suspicion that young Artemis Fowl wanted us to stop time. After all, everything else we've tried has played straight into his hands.'

Root rubbed his temples. 'That's impossible. How could a human know about time-stoppage? Anyway, this is no time for theorizing, Foaly. I have less than eight hours to clean up this mess. So what have you got for me?'

Foaly clopped over to an equipment rack clamped to the wall.

'No heavy armament, that's for sure. Not after what happened to Retrieval One. No helmet either. That beast of a Mud Man seems to collect them. No, to show good faith, we're going to send you in unarmed and unarmoured.'

Root snorted. 'What manual did you get this from?'

'It's standard operating procedure. Fostering trust speeds communication.'

'Oh, stop quoting and give me something to shoot.'

'Suit yourself,' sighed Foaly, selecting what looked like a finger from the rack.

'What's that?'

'It's a finger. What does it look like?'

'A finger,' admitted Root.

'Yes, but not any ordinary finger.' He glanced around to make sure that no one else was watching. 'The tip contains a pressurized dart. One shot only. You tap the knuckle with your thumb and someone goes sleepy-bye.'

'Why haven't I seen this before?'

'It's a covert kinda thing ...'

'And?' said Root suspiciously.

'Well, there have been accidents ...'

'Tell me, Foaly.'

'Our agents keep forgetting they have it on.'

'Meaning they shoot themselves.'

Foaly nodded miserably. 'One of our best sprites was picking his nose at the time. Three days on the critical list.'

Root rolled the *memory latex* on to his index finger, where it immediately assumed the shape and flesh tone of the host digit.

'Don't worry, Foaly, I'm not a complete idiot. Anything else?'

Foaly unhooked what appeared to be a false bottom

from the equipment rack.

'You're not serious! What does that do?'

'Nothing,' admitted the centaur. 'But it gets a great laugh at parties.'

Root chuckled. Twice. That was a major lapse for him.

'OK, levity over. Are you going to wire me?'

'Naturally. One iris-cam. What colour?' He peered into the commander's eyes. 'Hmm. Mud brown.' He selected a small vial from the shelf and removed the electronic contact lens from a fluid capsule. Plucking Root's eyelid with thumb and forefinger, he slotted in the iris-cam. 'That might irritate you. Try not to rub or it could end up in the back of your eye. Then we'd be looking into your head, and there's nothing interesting in there, heaven knows.'

Root blinked, resisting the urge to knead his watering eye.

'That's it?'

Foaly nodded. 'That's all we dare risk.'

The commander agreed reluctantly. His hip felt very light without a tri-barrelled blaster dangling from it.

'OK. I suppose this amazing dart finger will have to do. Honestly, Foaly, if this blows up in my face, you'll be on the next shuttle back to Haven.'

The centaur snickered. 'Just be careful in the toilet.'

Root didn't laugh. There were some things you didn't joke about.

*

Artemis's watch had stopped. It was as though Greenwich wasn't there any more. Or perhaps, mused Artemis, we're the ones who have disappeared. He checked CNN. It had frozen. A picture of Riz Khan jittered slightly on the screen. Artemis could not hold back a satisfied smile. They had done it, just like the Book said. The LEP had stopped time. All according to plan.

Time to check out a theory. Artemis wheeled over to the monitor bank and punched up the Mam Cam on the seventy-centimetre main monitor. Angeline Fowl was no longer on the chaise longue. Artemis panned around the room. It was empty. His mother had gone. Disappeared. His smile widened. Perfect. Just as he'd suspected.

Artemis switched his attention to Holly Short. She was banging the bed again. Occasionally she would rise from the mattress, pounding the wall with her bare fists. Maybe it was more than frustration. Could there be method in her madness? He tapped the monitor with a slim finger.

'What are you up to, Captain? What's your little plan?'

He was distracted by a movement on the avenue monitor.

'At last,' he breathed. 'The games begin.'

A figure was advancing down the avenue. Small, but imposing nonetheless. Unshielded too. Finished play-acting then.

Artemis punched the intercom button.

'Butler? We have a guest. I'll show him in. You get back here and police the surveillance cameras.'

Butler's voice came back tinny through the speaker.

'Ten four, Artemis. On my way.'

Artemis buttoned his designer jacket, pausing at the mirror to straighten his tie. The trick to negotiation was to hold all the cards going in and, even if you didn't, to try to look as though you did.

Artemis put on his best sinister face. Evil, he told himself, evil but highly intelligent. And determined, don't forget determined. He put a hand on the doorknob. Steady now. Deep breaths, and try not to think about the possibility that you have misjudged this situation and are about to be shot dead. One, two, three … He opened the door.

'Good evening,' he said, every inch the gracious host, albeit a sinister, evil, intelligent and determined one.

Root stood on the doorstep, palms up, the universal gesture for Look, I'm not carrying a big murderous weapon.

'You're Fowl?'

'Artemis Fowl, at your service. And you are?'

'LEP Commander Root. Right, we know each other's names, so could we get on with this?'

'Certainly.'

Root decided to chance his arm. 'Step outside then.

Where I can see you.'

Artemis's face hardened. 'Have you learned nothing from my demonstrations? The ship? Your commandos? Do I need to kill someone?'

'No,' said Root hurriedly. 'I only –'

'You only meant to lure me outside, where I could be snatched and used to trade. Please, Commander Root, raise your game or send someone intelligent.'

Root felt the blood pump through his cheeks.

'Now you just listen to me, you young ...'

Artemis smiled, in command again. 'Not very good negotiation techniques, Commander, to lose your cool before we even get to the table.'

Root took several deep breaths.

'Fine. Whatever you say. Where would you prefer to conduct our talks?'

'Inside of course. You have my permission to enter, but remember, Captain Short's life is in your hands. Be careful with it.'

Root followed his host down the vaulted hallway. Generations of Fowls glared down at him from classical portraits. They passed through a stained-oak doorway to a long conference room. There were two places set at a round table, complete with pads, ashtrays and water jugs.

Root was delighted to see the ashtrays and immediately pulled a half-chewed cigar from his vest.

'Maybe you're not such a barbarian after all,' he grunted, exhaling a huge cloud of green smoke. The commander ignored the water jugs, instead pouring himself a shot of something purple from a hip flask. He drank deeply, belched and sat.

'Ready?' Artemis shuffled his notes, like a newsreader. 'Here is the situation as I see it. I have the means to expose your subterranean existence, and you are powerless to stop me. So, basically, whatever I ask for is a small price to pay.'

Root spat out a shred of fungus tobacco. 'You think you can just put all this information out over the Internet.'

'Well, not immediately, not with the time-stop in effect.'

Root choked on a lungful of smoke. Their ace in the hole. Rumbled.

'Well, if you know about the time-stop, you must also know that you are completely cut off from the outside world. You are, in effect, powerless.'

Artemis jotted a note on the pad. 'Let's save some time here. I grow weary of your clumsy bluffs. In the case of an abduction, the LEP will first send a crack Retrieval team to get back what has been lost. You have done so. Excuse me while I titter. Crack team? Honestly. A Cub-Scout patrol armed with water pistols could have defeated them.'

Root fumed silently, taking out his anger on the cigar butt.

'The next official step is negotiation. And finally, when the eight-hours' time limit is about to run out, and if no solution can be reached, a bio-bomb is detonated, contained by the time-field.'

'You appear to know an awful lot about us, Master Fowl. I don't suppose you'll tell me how?'

'Correct.'

Root mashed the remains of his cigar into the crystal ashtray.

'So let's have it, what are your demands?'

'One demand. Singular.'

Artemis slid his notepad across the polished table. Root read what was written there.

'One tonne of twenty-four-carat gold. Small unmarked ingots only. You can't be serious.'

'Oh, but I am.'

Root sat forward in his chair. 'Don't you see? Your position is untenable. Either you give us back Captain Short or we will be forced to kill you all. There is no middle ground. We don't negotiate. Not really. I'm just here to explain the facts to you.'

Artemis smiled his vampire smile. 'Oh, but you will negotiate with me, Commander.'

'Oh, really? And what makes you so special?'

'I am special, because I know how to escape the time-field.'

'Impossible,' snorted Root. 'Can't be done.'

'Oh yes it can. Trust me, I haven't been wrong yet.'

Root tore off the top page, folding it into his pocket.

'I'll have to think about this.'

'Take your time. We have eight hours ... excuse me, seven and a half hours, then time's up for everybody.'

Root said nothing for a long while, tapping his nails on the tabletop. He took a breath to speak, then changed his mind and stood abruptly.

'We'll be in touch. Don't worry, I'll see myself out.'

Artemis pushed his chair back.

'You do that. But remember this, none of your race has permission to enter here while I'm alive.'

Root stalked down the hallway, glaring back at the oil paintings. Better to leave now and process this new information. The Fowl boy was indeed a slippery opponent. But he was making one basic mistake — the assumption that Root would play by the rules. However, Julius Root hadn't got his Commander's bars by following any rule book. Time for a bit of unorthodox action.

The videotape from Root's iris-cam was being reviewed by experts.

'You see there,' said Professor Cumulus, a behavioural specialist. 'That twitch, he's lying.'

'Nonsense,' huffed Doctor Argon, a psychologist from below the United States. 'He's itchy, that's all. He's itchy so he scratches. Nothing sinister in it.'

Cumulus turned to Foaly.

'Listen to him. How can I be expected to work with this charlatan?'

'Witch doctor,' countered Argon.

Foaly raised his hairy palms.

'Gentlemen, please. We need agreement here. A concrete profile.'

'It's no use,' said Argon. 'I can't work in these conditions.'

Cumulus folded his arms. 'If he can't work, neither can I.'

Root strode through the shuttle double doors. His trademark purple complexion was even rosier than usual.

'That human is toying with us. I will not have it. Now, what did our experts make of the tape?'

Foaly moved slightly to the side, allowing the commander a clear run at the so-called experts.

'Apparently they can't work in these conditions.'

Root's eyes narrowed to slits, bringing his prey into sharp focus. 'Excuse me?'

'The good doctor is a halfwit,' said Cumulus, unfamiliar with the commander's temper.

'I-I'm a halfwit?' stuttered Argon, equally ignorant. 'What about you, you cave fairy? Plastering your absurd interpretations on to the most innocent of gestures.'

'Innocent? The boy is a bag of nerves. Obviously lying. It's textbook.'

Root slammed a clenched fist on to the table, sending a spider's web of cracks scurrying across the surface.

'Silence!'

And silence there was. Instantly.

'Now, you two *experts* are on handsome retainers for your profiling work. Correct?'

The pair nodded, afraid to speak in case that broke the *silence* rule.

'This is probably the case of your lives, so I want you to concentrate very hard. Understood?'

More nods.

Root popped the camera out of his weeping eye.

'Fast-forward it, Foaly. Towards the end.'

The tape hopped forward erratically. On screen, Root followed the human into his conference room.

'There. Stop it there. Can you zoom in on his face?'

'Can I zoom in on his face?' snorted Foaly. 'Can a dwarf steal the web from under a spider?'

'Yes,' replied Root.

'That was a rhetorical question actually.'

'I don't need a grammar lesson, Foaly, just zoom in, would you?'

Foaly ground his tombstone teeth.

'OK, boss. Will do.'

The centaur's fingers prodded the keyboard with

lightning speed. Artemis's visage grew to fill the plasma screen.

'I'd advise you to listen,' said Root, squeezing the experts' shoulders. 'This is a pivotal moment in your careers.'

'I am special,' said the mouth on the screen, 'because I can escape the time-field.'

'Now tell me,' said Root. 'Is he lying?'

'Run it again,' said Cumulus. 'Show me the eyes.'

Argon nodded. 'Yes. Just the eyes.'

Foaly tapped a few more keys, and Artemis's deep blue eyes expanded to the width of the screen.

'I am special,' boomed the human voice, 'because I can escape the time-field.'

'Well, is he lying?'

Cumulus and Argon looked at each other, all traces of antagonism gone.

'No,' they said simultaneously.

'He's telling the truth,' added the behaviourist.

'Or,' clarified the psychologist, 'at least he thinks he is.'

Root swabbed his eye with a cleansing solution.

'That's what I thought. When I looked that human in the face, I figured he was either a genius or crazy.'

Artemis's cool eyes glared at them from the screen.

'So which is it?' asked Foaly. 'A genius or crazy?'

Root grabbed his tri-barrelled blaster from the gun rack.

'What's the difference?' he snapped, strapping his trusty weapon to his hip. 'Get me an outside line to E1. This Fowl person seems to know all of our rules, so it's time to break a few.'

CHAPTER 7: MULCH

 TIME to introduce a new character to our otherworldly pageant. Well, not strictly speaking a new character. We have encountered him before, in the LEP booking line. On remand for numerous larcenies: Mulch Diggums, the kleptomaniac dwarf. A dubious individual, even by Artemis Fowl's standards. As if this account didn't already suffer from an overdose of amoral individuals.

Born to a typical dwarf cavern-dwelling family, Mulch had decided early that mining was not for him and resolved to put his talents to another use, namely digging and entering, generally entering Mud People's property. Of course this meant forfeiting his magic. Dwellings were sacred. If you broke that rule, you had to be prepared to accept the consequences. Mulch didn't mind. He didn't care much for magic anyway. There had never been much use for it down the mines.

Things had gone pretty well for a few centuries, and

he'd built up quite a lucrative above-ground memorabilia business. That was until he'd tried to sell the Jules Rimet Cup to an undercover LEP operative. From then on his luck had turned, and he'd been arrested over twenty times to date. A total of 300 years in and out of prison.

Mulch had a prodigious appetite for tunnelling, and that, unfortunately, is a literal translation. For those unfamiliar with the mechanics of dwarf tunnelling, I shall endeavour to explain them as tastefully as possible. Like some members of the reptile family, dwarf males can unhinge their jaws, allowing them to ingest several kilos of earth a second. This material is processed by a super-efficient metabolism, stripped of any useful minerals and … ejected at the other end, as it were. Charming.

At present, Mulch was languishing in a stone-walled cell in LEP Central. At least, he was trying to project an image of a languishing, unperturbed kind of dwarf. Actually, he was quaking in his steel-toe-capped boots.

The goblin/dwarf turf war was flaring up at the moment and some bright spark LEP elf had seen fit to put him in a cell with a gang of psyched-up goblins. An oversight perhaps. More likely a spot of revenge for trying to pick his arresting officer's pocket in the booking line.

'So, dwarf,' sneered the head-honcho goblin, a wart-faced fellow covered in tattoos. 'How come you don't chew your way outta here?'

Mulch rapped on the walls. 'Solid rock.'

The goblin laughed. 'So what? Can't be any harder than your dwarf skull.'

His cronies laughed. So did Mulch. He thought it might be wise. Wrong.

'You laughin' at me, dwarf?'

Mulch stopped laughing.

'With you,' he corrected. 'I'm laughing with you. That skull joke was pretty funny.'

The goblin advanced until his slimy nose was a centimetre from Mulch's own. 'You pay-tron-izin' me, dwarf?'

Mulch swallowed, calculating. If he unhinged now, he could probably swallow the leader before the others reacted. Still, goblins were murder on the digestion. Very bony.

The goblin conjured up a fireball around his fist. 'I asked you a question, stumpy.'

Mulch could feel every sweat gland on his body pop into instant overdrive. Dwarfs did not like fire. They didn't even like thinking about flames. Unlike the rest of the fairy races, dwarfs had no desire to live above ground. Too close to the sun. Ironic for someone in the Mud People Possession Liberation business.

'N-no need for that,' he stammered. 'I was just trying to be friendly.'

'Friendly,' scoffed wart-face. 'Your kind don't know the meanin' of the word. Cowardly back-stabbers, the lot of you.'

Mulch nodded diplomatically. 'We have been known to be a bit treacherous.'

'A bit treacherous! A bit treacherous! My brother Phlegm was ambushed by a crowd of dwarfs disguised as dung heaps! He's still in traction!'

Mulch nodded sympathetically. 'The old dung heap ruse. Disgraceful. One of the reasons I don't associate with the Brotherhood.'

Wart-face twirled the fireball between his fingers. 'There are two things under this world that I really despise.'

Mulch had a feeling that he was about to find out what they were.

'One is a stinkin' dwarf.'

No surprises there.

'And the other is a traitor to his own kind. And from what I hear, you fall neatly into both categories.'

Mulch smiled weakly. 'Just my luck.'

'Luck ain't got nothin' to do with it. Fortune delivered you into my hands.'

On another day, Mulch might have pointed out that luck and fortune were basically the same thing. Not today.

'You like fire, dwarf?'

Mulch shook his head.

Wart-face grinned.

'Now ain't that a shame, 'cause any second now I'm going to ram this here fireball down your throat.'

The dwarf swallowed drily. Wasn't it just typical of the Dwarf Brotherhood? What do dwarfs hate? Fire. Who are the only creatures with the ability to conjure fireballs? Goblins. So who did the dwarfs pick a fight with? What a real no-brainer.

Mulch backed up to the wall.

'Careful there. We could all go up.'

'Not us,' grinned wart-face, snorting the fireball up two elongated nostrils. 'Completely fireproof.'

Mulch was perfectly aware what would happen next. He'd seen it too many times in the back alleys. A group of goblins would corner a stray brother dwarf, pin him down, and then the leader would give him the double barrels straight in the face.

Wart-face's nostrils quivered as he prepared to vent the inhaled fireball. Mulch quailed. There was only one chance. The goblins had made a basic mistake. They'd forgotten to pin his arms.

The goblin drew a breath through his mouth, then closed it. More exhalation pressure for the fire stream. He tilted his head back, pointing his nose at the dwarf, and let fly. Quick as a flash, Mulch jammed his thumbs up wart-face's nostrils. Disgusting, yes, but definitely better than being dwarf kebab.

The fireball had nowhere to go. It rebounded on the balls of Mulch's thumbs and ricocheted back into the goblin's head. The tear ducts provided the path of least

166

resistance, so the flames compressed into pressurized streams, erupting just below the goblin's eyes. A sea of flame spread across the cell roof.

Mulch withdrew his thumbs and, after a quick wipe, thrust them in his mouth, allowing the natural balm in his saliva to begin the healing process. Of course if he'd still had his magic, he could have just wished the scorched digits better. But that was the price you paid for a life of crime.

Wart-face didn't look so good. Smoke was leaking from every orifice in his head. Flameproof goblins may be, but the errant fireball had given his tubes a good scouring. He swayed like a strand of seaweed, then collapsed face down on the concrete floor. Something crunched. Probably a big goblin nose.

The other gang members did not react favourably.

'Look what he did to the boss!'

'That stinkin' stump.'

'Let's fry 'im.'

Mulch backed up even further. He'd been hoping the remaining goblins would lose their nerve once their leader was out of commission. Apparently not. Even though it was most definitely not in his nature, Mulch had no option but to attack.

He unhinged his jaw and leaped forward, clamping his teeth around the foremost goblin's head.

'Ow, bagg off!' he shouted around the obstruction in

his mouth. 'Bagg off or ur briend gedds it!'

The others froze, uncertain of their next move. Of course they'd all seen what dwarf molars could do to a goblin head. Not a pretty sight.

Each one popped a fireball in his fist.

'I'm warnih ooh!'

'You can't get us all, stumpy.'

Mulch resisted the impulse to bite down. It is the strongest of dwarf urges, a genetic memory born from millennia spent tunnelling. The fact that the goblin was wriggling slimily didn't help. His options were running out. The gang was advancing and he was powerless as long as his mouth was full. It was crunch time. Pardon the pun.

Suddenly the cell door clanked open and what seemed like an entire squadron of LEP officers flooded the confined space. Mulch felt the cold steel of a gun barrel against his temple.

'Spit out the prisoner,' ordered a voice.

Mulch was delighted to comply. A thoroughly slimed goblin collapsed retching on the floor.

'You goblins, put 'em out.'

One by one the fireballs were extinguished.

'That's not my fault,' whined Mulch, pointing to the spasming wart-face. 'He blew himself up.'

The officer holstered his weapon, drawing out a set of cuffs.

'I couldn't care less what you do to each other,' he said,

spinning Mulch and snapping the cuffs on. 'If it was up to me, I'd put the whole lot of you in a big room, and come back a week later to sluice it out. But Commander Root wants to see you above ground ASAP.'

'ASAP?'

'Now, if not sooner.'

Mulch knew Root. The commander was responsible for several of his government hotel visits. If Julius wanted to see him, it probably wasn't for drinks and a movie.

'Now? But it's daylight now. I'll burn.'

The LEP officer laughed.

'It ain't daylight where you're going, pal. Where you're going it ain't anything.'

Root was waiting for the dwarf inside the time-field portal. The portal was yet another of Foaly's inventions. Fairies could be introduced to and leave the time-field without affecting the altered flow inside the field. This effectively meant that even though it took nearly six hours to get Mulch to the surface, he was injected into the field only moments after Root had the notion to send for him.

It was Mulch's first time in a field. He stood watching life proceed at an exaggerated rate outside the shimmering corona. Cars zipped by at impossible speeds, and clouds tumbled across the skyline as though driven by force-ten gales.

'Mulch, you little reprobate,' roared Root. 'You can

take off that suit now. The field is UV-filtered, told.'

The dwarf had been issued a blackout suit at E1. E though dwarfs had thick skins, they were extremely sensitive to sunlight and had a burn time of less than three minutes. Mulch peeled off the skintight suit.

'Nice to see you, Julius.'

'That's Commander Root to you.'

'Commander now. I heard that. Clerical error, was it?'

Root's teeth ground his cigar to a pulp.

'I don't have time for this impudence, convict. And the only reason that my boot is not up your behind right now is that I have a job for you.'

Mulch frowned. 'Convict? I have a name, you know, Julius.'

Root squatted to the dwarf's level. 'I don't know what dreamworld you live in, convict, but in the real world you are a criminal and it is my job to ensure your life is as unpleasant as possible. So if you're expecting civility just because I've testified against you some fifteen times, forget it!'

Mulch rubbed his wrists where the handcuffs had left red welts.

'Fine, *Commander*. No need to blow a gasket. I'm not a murderer, you know, just a petty criminal.'

'From what I hear, you nearly made the transformation below in the cells.'

'Not my fault. They attacked me.'

Root screwed a fresh cigar into his mouth.

'Fine, whatever. Just follow me, and don't steal anything.'

'Yessir, Commander,' said Mulch innocently. He didn't need to steal anything else. He'd already palmed Root's field-access card when the commander had made the mistake of leaning over.

They crossed the Retrieval perimeter to the avenue.

'Do you see that manor?'

'What manor?'

Root rounded on him. 'I don't have time for this, convict. Nearly half my time-stop has elapsed. Another few hours and one of my best officers will be blue-rinsed!'

Mulch shrugged. 'None of my concern. I'm just a criminal, remember. And by the way, I know what you want me to do, and the answer is no.'

'I haven't even asked you yet.'

'It's obvious. I'm a housebreaker. That's a house. You can't go in because you'll lose your magic, but my magic is already gone. Two and two.'

Root spat out the cigar. 'Don't you have any civic pride? Our entire way of life is on the line here.'

'Not my way of life. Fairy prison, human prison. It's all the same to me.'

The commander thought about it.

⚶ℬⱳ · ⍜ · ⱳ⍜⍀⍀ · ⊞⍓ · ⍼⍜⍜⊞ ·

'OK, you slime. Fifty years off your sentence.'

'I want amnesty.'

'In your dreams, Mulch.'

'Take it or leave it.'

'Seventy-five years in minimum security. *You* take it or leave it.'

Mulch pretended to think. It was all academic, seeing as he intended escaping anyway.

'Single cell?'

'Yes, yes. Single cell. Now, will you do it?'

'Very well, Julius. Only because it's you.'

Foaly was searching for a matching iris-cam.

'Hazel, I think. Or perhaps tawny. You really do have stunning eyes, Mister Mulch.'

'Thank you, Foaly. My mother always said they were my most attractive feature.'

Root was pacing the shuttle floor.

'You two do realize we're on a deadline here, don't you? Never mind matching the colour. Just give him a camera.'

Foaly plucked a lens from its solution with tweezers.

'This is not just vanity, Commander. The closer the match, the less interference from the actual eye.'

'Whatever, whatever, just get on with it.'

Foaly grabbed Mulch's chin, holding him still.

'There you are. We're with you all the way.'

Foaly twisted a tiny cylinder into the thick tufts of hair growing from Mulch's ear.

'Wired for sound now too. In case you need to call for assistance.'

The dwarf smiled wryly. 'Forgive me for not swelling with confidence. I find I've always done better on my own.'

'If you can call seventeen convictions doing better,' chuckled Root.

'Oh, we have time for jokes now, do we?'

Root grabbed him by the shoulder. 'You're right. We don't. Let's go.'

He dragged Mulch across a grassy verge to a cluster of cherry trees.

'I want you to tunnel in there and find out how this Fowl person knows so much about us. Probably some surveillance device. Whatever it is, destroy it. Find Captain Short if possible and see what you can do for her. If she is dead, at least it will clear the way for a bio-bomb.'

Mulch squinted across the landscape. 'I don't like it.'

'What don't you like?'

'The lie of the land. I smell limestone. Solid-rock foundation. There might not be a way in.'

Foaly trotted across. 'I've done a scan. The original structure is based totally on rock, but some of the later extensions stray on to clay. The wine cellar in the south wing appears to have a wooden floor. It should be no problem for someone with a mouth like yours.'

Mulch decided to take that as a statement of fact rather than an insult. He opened the bum-flap on his tunnelling trousers. 'Right. Stand back.'

Root and the surrounding LEP officers rushed for cover, but Foaly, who had never actually seen a dwarf tunnelling, decided to stay for a peek.

'Good luck, Mulch.'

The dwarf unhinged his jaw.

'Ank oo,' he mumbled, bending over for launch.

The centaur looked around.

'Where's everyone —'

He never finished that statement, because a blob of recently swallowed and even more recently recycled clay whacked him in the face. By the time he'd cleared his eyes, Mulch had disappeared down a vibrating hole, and there was the sound of hearty laughter shaking the cherry trees.

Mulch followed a loamy vein through a volcanic fold in the rock. Nice consistency, not too many loose stones. Plenty of insect life too. Vital for strong healthy teeth, a dwarf's most important attribute — the first thing a prospective mate looked at. Mulch went low to the limestone, his belly almost scraping the rock. The deeper the tunnel, the less chance of subsidence on the surface. You couldn't be too careful these days, not with motion sensors and landmines. Mud People went to extraordinary lengths to protect their valuables. With good reason, as it happened.

Mulch felt a vibration cluster to his left. Rabbits. The dwarf fixed the location in his internal compass. Always useful to know where the local wildlife hung out. He skirted the warren, following the manor foundations around in a long north-westerly loop.

Wine cellars were easy to locate. Over the centuries, residue seeped through the floor, infusing the land beneath with the wine's personality. This one was sombre, nothing cheeky here. A touch of fruit, but not enough to lighten the flavour. Definitely an occasion wine on the bottom rack. Mulch burped. That was good clay.

The dwarf aimed his scything jaws skywards, punching through the floorboards. He hauled himself through the jagged hole, shaking the last of the recycled mud from his trousers.

He was in a blessedly dark room, perfect for dwarf vision. His sonar had guided him to an uncovered spot in the floor. One metre to the left and he would have emerged in a huge barrel of Italian red.

Mulch rehinged his jaw and padded across to the wall. He flattened a conch-like ear to the red brickwork. For a moment he was absolutely still, absorbing the house's vibrations. A lot of low-frequency humming. There was a generator somewhere, and plenty of juice running through the wires.

Footsteps too. Way up. Maybe on the third floor. And close by. A crashing sound. Metal on concrete. There it was again. Someone was building something. Or breaking something down.

Something skittered past his foot. Mulch squashed it instinctively. It was a spider. Just a spider.

'Sorry, little friend,' he said to the grey smear. 'I'm a bit on the jittery side.'

The steps were wooden, of course. More than a century old too by the smell of them. Steps like that creaked as soon as you looked at them. Better than any pressure pads for giving away intruders. Mulch climbed along the edges, one foot in front of the other. Right in by the wall was where the wood had most support and was less likely to creak.

This was not as simple as it sounds. Dwarf feet are designed for spadework, not for the delicate intricacies of ballet dancing or balancing on wooden steps. Nonetheless, Mulch reached the door without incident. A couple of minor squeaks, but nothing that would be detectable by human ears or hardware.

The door was locked, naturally, but it may as well not have been for all the challenge it presented to a kleptomaniac dwarf.

Mulch reached into his beard, plucking out a sturdy hair. Dwarf hair is radically different from the human variety. Mulch's beard and head hair were actually a matrix of antennae that helped him to navigate and avoid danger below ground. Once removed from its pore, the hair immediately stiffened in rapid rigor mortis. Mulch twisted the end in the seconds before it became completely rigid. A perfect pick.

One quick jiggle and the lock yielded. Only two tumblers. Terrible security. Typical of humans, they never expected an attack from below. Mulch stepped on to a parquet corridor. The whole place smelled of money. He could make a fortune here, if only he had the time.

There were cameras just below the architrave. Tastefully done, nestling in the natural shadows. But vigilant none the less. Mulch stood for a moment, calculating the system's blindspot. Three cameras on the corridor. Ninety-second sweep. No way through.

'You could ask for help?' said a voice in his ear.

'Foaly?' Mulch pointed his wired eyeball at the nearest camera. 'Can you do anything about those?' he whispered.

The dwarf heard the sound of a keyboard being manipulated, and suddenly his right eye zoomed like a camera lens.

'Handy,' breathed Mulch. 'I've got to get me one of these.'

Root's voice crackled through the tiny speaker. 'No chance, convict. Government issue. Anyway, what would you do with one in prison? Get a close-up of the other side of your cell?'

'You're such a charmer, Julius. What's the matter? Are you jealous because I'm succeeding where you failed?'

Root's foul swearing was drowned out by Foaly.

'OK, I've got it. Simple video network. Not even digital. I'm going to broadcast a loop of the last ten seconds to every camera through our dishes. That should give you a few minutes.'

Mulch shuffled uncomfortably. 'How long will that take? I'm a bit exposed here, you know.'

'It's already started,' replied Foaly. 'So get moving.'

'Are you sure?'

'Of course I'm sure. Elementary electronics. I've been messing with human surveillance since kindergarten. You'll just have to trust me.'

I'd rather trust a bunch of humans not to hunt a species to extinction than trust an LEP consultant, thought Mulch. But aloud he said, 'OK. I'm away. Over and out.'

He sneaked down the hall. Even his hands were sneaky, padding the air as if he could somehow make himself lighter. Whatever that centaur did must have worked, because there were no agitated Mud People racing down the stairs, waving primitive gunpowder weapons.

Stairs. Ah, stairs. Mulch had a thing for stairs. They were like predug shafts. He found that inevitably the best booty lay at their summit. And what a stairway. Stained oak, with the intricate carvings generally associated with either the eighteenth century or the obscenely rich.

Mulch rubbed his finger along an ornate banister. In this case, probably both.

Still, no time to moon about. Stairways did not tend to remain deserted for long, especially during a siege. Who could tell how many bloodthirsty troopers waited behind each door, eager for a fairy head to add to their stuffed trophy wall.

Mulch climbed carefully, taking nothing for granted. Even solid oak creaked. He stuck to the borders, avoiding the carpet inlay. The dwarf knew from conviction number eight how easy it was to conceal a pressure pad beneath the deep shag of some antique weave.

He reached the landing with his head still attached to his shoulders. But there was another problem quite literally brewing. Dwarf digestion, due to its accelerated rate, can be quite explosive. The loosely packed soil on the Fowl estate was very well aerated and a lot of that air had entered Mulch's tubes along with the soil and minerals. Now the air wanted to get out.

Dwarf etiquette dictated that gas be passed while still in the tunnel, but Mulch didn't have time for manners. Now he regretted not taking a moment to get rid of the gas while he was in the cellar. The problem with dwarf gas was that it couldn't go up, only down. Imagine, if you will, the catastrophic effects of burping while digesting a mouthful of clay. Total system back-up. Not a pretty sight. Thus dwarf anatomy ensured that all gas was passed below, actually aiding in the expulsion of unwanted clay. Of course, there's a simpler way of putting this, but that version can only be read in the adult book.

Mulch wrapped his arms around his stomach. He'd better get out of the open. A blowout on a landing like this could take out the windows. He shuffled along the corridor, skipping through the first doorway he encountered.

More cameras. Quite a lot of them, in fact. Mulch studied the lenses' sweep. Four were surveying the general floorspace, but another three were fixed.

'Foaly? You there?' whispered the dwarf.

'No!' The typical sarcastic reply. 'I have much better things to do than worry about the collapse of civilization as we know it.'

'Yes, thank you. Don't let my life being in danger interrupt your merriment.'

'I'll try not to.'

'I have a challenge for you.'

Foaly was instantly interested. 'Really? Go on.'

Mulch pointed his gaze at the recessed cameras, half hidden in the swirling architrave. 'I need to know where those three cameras are pointing. Exactly.'

Foaly laughed. 'That's not a challenge. Those old video systems emit faint ion beams. Invisible to the naked eye, of course, but not with your iris-cam.'

The hardware in Mulch's eye flickered and sparked.

180

'Oww!'

'Sorry. Small charge.'

'You could have warned me.'

'I'll give you a big kiss later, you baby. I thought dwarfs were tough.'

'We are tough. I'll show you just how tough when I get back.'

Root's voice interrupted the posturing. 'You won't be showing anyone anything, convict, except perhaps where the toilet is in your cell. Now, what do you see?'

Mulch looked at the room again through his ion-sensitive eye. Each camera was emitting a faint beam, like the last evening sunrays. The rays pooled on a portrait of Artemis Fowl Senior.

'Not behind the picture. Oh, please.'

Mulch placed his ear against the picture glass. Nothing electrical. Not alarmed then. Just to be sure, he sniffed the frame's edge. No plastic or copper. Wood, steel and glass. Some lead in the paint. He curled a nail behind the frame and pulled. The picture came away smoothly, hinged on the side. And behind it. A safe.

'It's a safe,' said Foaly.

'I know that, you idiot. I'm trying to concentrate here! If you want to help, tell me the combination.'

'No problem. Oh, by the way, there's another little shock coming. Maybe the big baby would like to suck his thumb for comfort.'

'Foaly. I'm going to … Owww!'

'There. That's the X-ray on.'

Mulch squinted at the safe. It was incredible. He could see right into the works. Tumblers and catches stood out in shadowy relief. He blew on his hairy fingers and twisted the combination dial. In seconds the safe lay open before him.

'Oh,' he said, disappointed.

'What is it?'

'Nothing. Just human currency. Nothing of value.'

'Leave it,' ordered Root. 'Try another room. Get going.'

Mulch nodded. Another room. Before his time ran out. But something was niggling at him. If this guy was so clever, why did he put the safe behind a painting? Such a cliché. Totally against form. No. Something wasn't right here. They were being duped somehow.

Mulch closed the safe, swinging the portrait back into position. It swung smoothly, weightless on the hinges. Weightless. He swung the picture out again. And back in.

'Convict. What are you doing?'

'Shut up, Julius! I mean, quiet a moment, Commander.'

Mulch squinted at the frame's profile. A bit thicker than normal. Quite a bit thicker. Even taking the box frame into account. Five centimetres. He ran a nail down the heavy cartridge backing and stripped it away to reveal …

'Another safe.'

A smaller one. Custom-made, obviously.

'Foaly. I can't see through this.'

'Lead-lined. You're on your own, burglar boy. Do what you do best.'

'Typical,' muttered Mulch, flattening his ear to the cold steel.

He twirled the dial experimentally. Nice action. The clicks were muted by the lead, he would have to concentrate. The upside was that something this thin could have only three tumblers at the most.

Mulch held his breath and twisted the dial, one cog at a time. To the normal ear, even with amplification, the clicks would have seemed uniform. But to Mulch, each cog had a distinctive signature and when a ratchet caught, it was so loud as to be deafening.

'One,' he breathed.

'Hurry it up, convict. Your time is running out.'

'You interrupted to tell me that? I can see now how you made commander, Julius.'

'Convict. I'm going to …'

But it was no use. Mulch had removed his earpiece, slipping it into his pocket. Now he could devote his full attention to the task at hand.

'Two.'

There was noise outside. In the hall. Someone was coming. About the size of an elephant by the size of it. No doubt this was the man mountain that had made mincemeat of the Retrieval Squad.

Mulch blinked a bead of sweat from his eye. Concentrate. Concentrate. The cogs clicked by. Millimetre by millimetre. Nothing was catching. The floor seemed to be hopping gently, though he could be imagining it.

Click, click. Come on. Come on. His fingers were slick with perspiration, the dial slipping between them. Mulch wiped them on his jerkin.

'Now, baby, come on. Talk to me.'

Click. Thunk.

'Yes!'

Mulch twisted the handle. Nothing. Still an obstruction. He ran a fingertip over the metal face. There. A small irregularity. A micro keyhole. Too small for your average lock pick. Time for a little trick he'd learned in prison. Quickly though, his stomach was bubbling like stew in the oven, and the footsteps were getting closer.

Selecting a sturdy chin hair, Mulch fed it gently into the tiny hole. When the tip reappeared, he pulled the root from his chin. The hair immediately stiffened, retaining the shape of the lock's interior.

Mulch held his breath and twisted. Smooth as a goblin's lie, the lock opened. Beautiful. At moments like these, it was almost worth all the jail time.

The kleptomaniac dwarf swung back the little door.

Beautiful work. Almost worthy of a fairy forge. Light as a wafer. Inside was a small chamber. And in the chamber was …

'Oh, gods above,' breathed Mulch.

Then things came to a head rather rapidly. The shock that Mulch had experienced communicated itself to his bowels, and they decided the excess air had got to go. Mulch knew the symptoms. Jelly legs, bubbling cramps, wobbly behind. In the seconds remaining to him, he snatched the object from the safe and, leaning over, he clasped his knees for support.

The constrained wind had built itself up to mini-cyclone intensity and could not be constrained. And so it exited. Rather abrasively. Blowing open Mulch's bum-flap and slamming into the rather large gentleman who had been sneaking up behind him.

Artemis was glued to the monitors. This was the time when things traditionally went wrong for kidnappers — the third quarter of operations. Having been successful thus far, the abductors tended to relax, light up a few cigarettes, get chatty with their hostages. Next thing they knew, they were flat on their faces with a dozen guns pointed at the backs of their heads. Not Artemis Fowl. He didn't make mistakes.

No doubt the fairies were reviewing the tapes of their first negotiating session, searching for anything that would give them a way in. Well, it was there all right. All they had to do was look. Buried just deep enough to make it look accidental.

It was possible that Commander Root would try another ruse. He was a wily one, no doubt about it. One who would not take kindly to being bested by a child. He would bear watching.

The mere thought of Root gave Artemis the shivers. He decided to check in again. He inspected the monitors.

Juliet was still in the kitchen, scrubbing at the sink. Washing the vegetables.

Captain Short was on her bunk. Quiet as the grave. No more bed banging. Perhaps he had been wrong about her. Perhaps there was no plan.

Butler stood at his post outside Holly's cell. Odd. He should have been on his rounds by now. Artemis grabbed a walkie-talkie.

'Butler?'

'Roger, base. Receiving.'

'Shouldn't you be on your rounds?'

There was a pause. 'I am, Artemis. Patrolling the main landing. Coming up on the safe room. I'm waving at you right now.'

Artemis glanced at the landing cameras. Deserted. From every angle. Definitely no waving manservant. He studied the monitors, counting under his breath ... There! Every ten seconds, a slight jump. On every screen.

'A loop!' he cried, jumping from his chair. 'They're feeding us a loop!'

Over the speaker, he could hear Butler's pace quickening to a run.

'The safe room!'

Artemis's stomach dropped into queasy hell. Duped! He, Artemis Fowl, had been duped, even though he'd known it was coming. Inconceivable. It was arrogance that had done it. His own blinding arrogance, and now the entire plan could collapse around his ears.

He switched the walkie-talkie to Juliet's band. It was a pity now that he'd taken the house's intercom off-line, but it didn't operate on a secure frequency.

'Juliet?'

'Receiving.'

'Where are you right now?'

'In the kitchen. Wrecking my nails on this grater.'

'Leave it, Juliet. Check on the prisoner.'

'But, Artemis, the carrot sticks will dry out!'

'Leave it, Juliet!' shouted Artemis. 'Drop everything and check on the prisoner!'

Juliet obediently dropped everything, including the walkie-talkie. She'd sulk for days now. Never mind. There was no time to worry about a teenage girl's bruised ego. He had more important matters to tend to.

Artemis depressed the master switch on the computerized surveillance system. His only chance of purging the loop was a complete reboot. After several agonizing moments of screen snow, the monitors jumped and settled. Things were not as they had seemed only seconds before.

There was a grotesque *thing* in the safe room. It had apparently discovered the secret compartment. Not only that but it had managed to open the whisper lock. Amazing. Butler had it covered though. He was sneaking up behind the creature, and any moment now the intruder would find itself nose down in the carpet.

Artemis switched his attention to Holly. The elf was back to bed banging. Slamming the frame down over and over again, as though she could …

It hit Artemis then, like a blast from a water cannon. If Holly had somehow smuggled an acorn in here, then one square centimetre of ground would be enough. If Juliet left that door open …

'Juliet!' he shouted into the walkie-talkie. 'Juliet! Don't go in there!'

But it was useless. The girl's walkie-talkie lay buzzing on the kitchen floor, and Artemis could only watch helplessly as Butler's sister strode towards the cell door, muttering about carrots.

'The safe room!' exclaimed Butler, quickening his pace. His instinct was to go in all guns blazing, but training took over. Fairy hardware was most definitely superior to his own, and who knew how many barrels were aimed at the other side of that door right now. No, caution was most definitely the best part of valour in this particular situation.

He placed a palm against the wood, feeling for vibration. Nothing. No machinery then. Butler curled his fingers around the knob, twisting gently. With his other hand, he drew a Sig Sauer automatic from his shoulder holster. No time to fetch the dart rifle, it would have to be shoot to kill.

The door swung open noiselessly, as Butler knew it would, having oiled every hinge in the house himself. Before him was ... Well, to be honest, Butler wasn't quite sure what it was. If he didn't know better, that is at first glance, he could have sworn that the thing resembled nothing more than an enormous quivering ...

And then the *thing* exploded, jettisoning an amazing amount of tunnel waste directly at the unfortunate manservant! It was like being battered with a hundred sledgehammers simultaneously. Butler was lifted bodily and flung against the wall.

And as he lay there, consciousness slipping away from him, he prayed that Master Artemis hadn't managed to capture the moment on video.

*

Holly was weakening. The bedframe was nearly twice her body weight and the ridges were tearing cruel welts in her palms. But she couldn't stop now. Not when she was so close.

She slammed the post into the concrete again. A cloud of grey dust spiralled around her legs. Any second now, Fowl would tumble to her plan and she'd get the hypodermic treatment again. But until then …

She gritted her teeth against the pain, heaving the bedframe to knee height. Then she saw it. A sliver of brown among the grey. Could it be true?

Pain forgotten, Captain Short dropped the bed, sinking quickly to her knees. There was indeed a small patch of earth poking through the cement. Holly fumbled the acorn from her boot, clasping it tightly in bloody fingers.

'I return you to the earth,' she whispered, worming her fist into the tiny space. 'And claim the gift that is my right.'

Nothing happened for a heartbeat. Perhaps two. Then Holly felt the magic rush up her arm like a jolt from an electrified troll fence. The shock sent her spinning across the room. For a moment the world swirled in a disconcerting kaleidoscope of colour, but when it settled Holly was no longer the defeated elf she had been.

'Right, Master Fowl.' She grinned, watching the blue sparks of fairy magic seal her wounds. 'Let's see what I have to do to get your permission to leave this place.'

*

'Drop everything,' sulked Juliet. 'Drop everything and check the prisoner.' She flicked blonde tresses expertly over a shoulder. 'He must think I'm his maid or something.'

She hammered on the cell door with the flat of her hand.

'I'm coming in now, fairy girl, so if you're doing anything embarrassing, please stop.'

Juliet punched the combination into the keypad. 'And no, I don't have your vegetables, or your washed fruit. But it's not my fault, Artemis *in-sis-ted* I come right down ...'

Juliet stopped talking, because there was nobody listening. She was preaching to an empty room. She waited for her brain to pass on an explanation. Nothing came. Eventually the notion to take another look filtered down.

She took a tentative step into the concrete cube. Nothing. Only a slight shimmering in the shadows. Like a mist. It was probably these stupid glasses. How were you supposed to see anything wearing mirrored sunglasses underground? And they were so nineties, they weren't even retro yet.

Juliet glanced guiltily at the monitor. Just a quick peek, what harm could it do? She whipped up the frames, sending her eyeballs spinning around the room.

In that instant a figure materialized before her. Just

stepped out of the air. It was Holly. She was smiling.

'Oh, it's you. How did you —'

The fairy interrupted with a wave of her hand.

'Why don't you take off those glasses, Juliet? They really don't suit you.'

She's right, thought Juliet. And what a lovely voice. Like a choir all on its own. How could you argue with a voice like that?

'Sure. Caveman glasses off. Cool voice, by the way. Doh ray me and all that.'

Holly decided not to try deciphering Juliet's comments. It was hard enough when the girl was in full control of her brain.

'Now. A simple question.'

'No problem.' What a great idea.

'How many people in the house?'

Juliet thought. One and one and one.

And another one? No, Mrs Fowl wasn't there.

'Three,' she said finally. 'Me and Butler and, of course, Artemis. Mrs Fowl was here, but she went bye-bye, then she went bye-bye.'

Juliet giggled. She'd made a joke. A good one too.

Holly drew a breath to ask for clarification, then thought better of it. A mistake as it turned out.

'Has anyone else been here. Anyone like me?'

Juliet chewed her lip. 'There was one little man. In a uniform like yours. Not cute though. Not one bit. Just shouted and smoked a smelly cigar. Terrible complexion. Red as a tomato.'

Holly almost smiled. Root had come himself. No doubt the negotiations had been disastrous.

'No one else?'

'Not that I know of. If you see that man again, tell him to lay off the red meat. He's just a coronary waiting to happen.'

Holly swallowed a grin. Juliet was the only human she knew who was probably more lucid under the *mesmer*.

'OK. I'll tell him. Now, Juliet, I want you to stay in my room, and no matter what you hear, don't come out.'

Juliet frowned. 'This room? It's so boring. No TV or anything. Can't I go up to the lounge?'

'No. You have to stay here. Anyway, they've just installed a wall television. Cinema size. Wrestling, twenty-four hours a day.'

Juliet almost fainted with pleasure. She ran into the cell, gasping as her imagination supplied the pictures.

Holly shook her head. Well, she thought, at least one of us is happy.

Mulch gave his rear end a shake to dislodge any clumps of earth. If only his mother could see him now, spraying mud on the Mud People. That was irony, or something like it. Mulch had never been big on grammar in school. That or poetry. He'd never seen the point. Down the mines, there were only two phrases of any importance: 'Look, gold!' and 'Cave in, everybody out!' No hidden meanings there, or rhymes.

The dwarf buttoned his bum-flap, which had been blasted open by the gale emanating from his nether regions. Time to make a run for it. Whatever hope he'd had of escaping undiscovered had been blown. Literally.

Mulch retrieved his earpiece, screwing it firmly into his ear. Well, you never knew, even the LEP might prove useful.

'... And when I get my hands on you, convict, you'll wish you stayed down those mines ...'

Mulch sighed. Ah well. Nothing new there then.

Clasping the safe's treasure tightly in his fist, the dwarf turned to retrace his steps. To his utter amazement there was a human entangled in the banisters. Mulch was not one bit surprised that his recyclings had managed to hurl the elephantine Mud Man several metres through the air. Dwarf gas had been known to cause avalanches in the Alps. What did surprise him was the fact that the man had managed to get so close to him in the first place.

'You're good,' said Mulch, wagging a finger at the unconscious bodyguard. 'But nobody takes a body blow from Mulch Diggums and stays on their feet.'

The Mud Man stirred, the whites of his eyes showing beneath fluttering lids.

Root's voice crackled in the dwarf's ears. 'Get a move on, Mulch *Diggums,* before that Mud Man gets up and rearranges your innards. He took out an entire Retrieval team, you know.'

Mulch swallowed, his bravado suddenly deserting him.

'An *entire* Retrieval team? Maybe I should get back underground … for the good of the mission.'

Skipping hurriedly around the groaning bodyguard, Mulch took the steps two at a time. No point in worrying about creaking stairs when you've just sent the intestinal equivalent of Hurricane Hal scurrying around the corridors.

He'd almost reached the cellar door when a figure shimmered into focus before him. Mulch recognized it as his arresting officer from the Renaissance Masters smuggling case.

'Captain Short.'

'Mulch. I wasn't expecting to see you.'

The dwarf shrugged. 'Julius had a dirty job. Someone had to do it.'

'I get it,' said Holly, nodding. 'You've already lost your magic. Smart. What did you find out?'

Mulch showed Holly his find. 'This was in his safe.'

'A copy of the Book!' gasped Holly. 'No wonder we're in this fix. We were playing into his hands all along.'

Mulch opened the cellar door. 'Shall we?'

'I can't. I'm under eyeball orders not to leave the house.'

'You magical types and your rituals. You have no idea how liberating it is to be rid of all that mumbo-jumbo.'

A series of sharp noises drifted down from the upper landing. It sounded like a troll thrashing around in a crystal emporium.

'We can debate ethics at a later date. Right now I suggest we make ourselves scarce.'

Mulch nodded. 'Agreed. This guy took out an entire Retrieval squad apparently.'

Holly paused, half shielded.

'An entire squad? Hmm. Fully equipped. I wonder ...'

She continued her fade-out, and the last thing to go was her widening grin.

Mulch was tempted to hang around. There weren't many things more fun to watch than a heavily armed Recon officer going to town on a bunch of unsuspecting humans. By the time Captain Short got through with this Fowl character, he'd be begging her to get out of his manor.

The Fowl character in question was watching it all from the surveillance room. There was no denying it. Things were not good. Not good at all. But certainly not irredeemable. There was still hope.

Artemis catalogued the events of the last few minutes.

The manor's security had been compromised. The safe room was in a shambles, blown apart by some sort of fairy flatulence. Butler lay unconscious, possibly paralysed by the same gaseous anomaly. His hostage was loose in the house, her fairy powers restored to her. There was an unsightly creature in leather chaps burrowing holes beneath the foundations, with no apparent regard for the fairy commandments. And the People had retrieved a copy of the Book, one of several copies as it happened, including one on disk in a Swiss vault.

Artemis's finger combed an errant strand of dark hair. He would have to dig very deep to uncover the good in this particular scenario. He took several deep breaths, finding his *chi* as Butler had taught him.

After several moments' contemplation, he realized that these factors meant little to the overall strategies of both sides. Captain Short was still trapped in the manor. And the time-stoppage period was running out. Soon the LEP would have no option but to launch their bio-bomb, and that was when Artemis Fowl would unveil his coup de grâce. Of course, the whole thing depended on Commander Root. If Root was as intellectually challenged as he looked, it was quite possible the entire scheme would collapse around his ears. Artemis hoped fervently that someone on the fairy team had the wit to spot the 'blunder' he'd made during the negotiation session.

*

Mulch unbuttoned his bum-flap. Time to suck some dirt, as they said down the mines. The trouble with dwarf tunnels was that they were self-sealing, so that if you had to go back the way you came, there was a whole new burrow to be excavated. Some dwarfs retraced their steps exactly, chewing through the less compact and pre-digested dirt. Mulch preferred to dig a fresh tunnel. For some reason, eating the same dirt twice didn't appeal to him.

Unhinging his jaw, the dwarf pointed himself torpedo-like through the hole in the floorboards. His heart calmed immediately as the scent of minerals filled his nostrils. Safe, he was safe. Nothing could catch a dwarf underground, not even a Skaylian rock worm. That was, of course, if he managed to get underground …

Ten very powerful fingers gripped Mulch by the ankles. This just wasn't the dwarf's day. First wart-face, now this homicidal human. Some people never learn. Usually Mud People.

'Egg go,' he mumbled, unhinged jaw flapping uselessly.

'Not a chance,' came the reply. 'The only way you're leaving this house is in a body bag.'

Mulch could feel himself being dragged backwards. This human was strong. There weren't many creatures that could dislodge a dwarf with a grip on something. He scrabbled in the dirt, cramming handfuls of wine-impregnated clay into his cavernous mouth. There was only one chance.

'Come on, you little goblin. Out of there.'

Goblin! Mulch would have been indignant had he not been busy chewing clay to eject at his enemy.

The human stopped talking. Possibly he had noticed the bum-flap, and probably the bum. No doubt what had happened in the safe room was coming back to him.

'Oh ...'

What would have followed the 'Oh' is anyone's guess, but I'd be willing to bet that it wouldn't have been 'dearie me'. As it happened, Butler never had time to finish his expletive, because he wisely chose that moment to relinquish his grip. A wise choice indeed, because it coincided with the instant Mulch decided to launch his earthen offensive.

A lump of compacted clay sped like a cannonball directly at the spot where Butler's head had been barely a second previously. Had it still occupied that space, the impact would have separated it from Butler's shoulders. An ignoble end for a bodyguard of his calibre. As it was, the soggy missile barely grazed his ear. Nevertheless, the force was sufficient to spin Butler like an ice skater, landing him on his rump for the second time in as many minutes.

By the time his vision had settled, the dwarf had

disappeared into a maelstrom of churning muck. Butler decided not to attempt pursuit. Dying below ground was not very high on his *things to do* list. But there will be another day, fairy, he thought grimly. And there was to be. But that's another story.

Mulch's momentum propelled him underground. He'd gone several metres along the loamy vein before he realized no one was following. Once the taste of earth had settled his heart rate, he decided it was time to implement his escape plan.

The dwarf altered his course, chewing his way towards the rabbit warren he'd noted earlier. With any luck, the centaur hadn't run a seismology test on the manor grounds, or his ruse might be discovered. He'd just have to bank on the fact that they had more important things to worry about than a missing prisoner. There shouldn't be any problem deceiving Julius, but the centaur, he was a smart one.

Mulch's internal compass steered him true, and within minutes he could feel the gentle vibrations of the rabbits loping along their tunnels. From here on timing was crucial if the illusion was to be effective. He slowed his digging rate, poking the soft clay gently until his fingers breached the tunnel wall. Mulch was careful to look the other way, because whatever he saw would be showing up on the viewscreen back in LEP HQ.

Laying his fingers on the tunnel floor like an upturned spider, Mulch waited. It didn't take long. In seconds he felt the rhythmic thump of an approaching rabbit. The instant the animal's hind legs brushed the trap, he tightened his powerful digits around its neck. The poor animal never had a chance.

Sorry, friend, thought the dwarf. If there was any other way ... Pulling the rabbit's body through the hole, Mulch rehinged his jaw and began screaming. 'Cave in! Cave in! Help! Help!'

Now for the tricky bit. With one hand he agitated the surrounding earth, bringing showers of it crumbling around his own head. With the other hand he popped the iris-cam out of his left eye and slid it into the rabbit's. Given the almost total darkness and the landfall confusion, it should be almost impossible to spot the switch.

'Julius! Please. Help me.'

'Mulch! What's happening? What's your status?'

What's my status? thought the dwarf incredulously. Even in times of supposed crisis, the commander couldn't abandon his precious protocol.

'I ... Argh ...' The dwarf dragged his final scream out, petering off to a gargling rattle.

A bit melodramatic perhaps, but Mulch never could resist theatrics. With a last regretful glance at

the dying animal, he unhinged his jaw and finned off
to the south-east. Freedom beckoned.

⊕◻◊•◔♈•♐•⋃◻♐⋃•⊕◻♐⊕•◻•

CHAPTER 8: TROLL

 ROOT leaned forward, roaring into the microphone. 'Mulch! What's happening? What's your status?'

Foaly was tapping a keyboard furiously.

'We've lost audio. Motion too.'

'Mulch. Talk to me, dammit.'

'I'm running a scan on his vitals … Woah!'

'What? What is it?'

'His heart has gone crazy. Beating like a rabbit …'

'A rabbit?'

'No, wait, it's …'

'What?' breathed the commander, terribly afraid that he already knew.

Foaly leaned back in his chair. 'It's stopped. His heartbeat has stopped.'

'Are you sure?'

'The monitors don't lie. All vitals can be read through the iris-cam. Not a peep. He's gone.'

𝄞𝄞𝄞 • 𝄞𝄞𝄞𝄞𝄞𝄞 ➔ • 𝄞𝄞𝄞 • 𝄞 • 𝄞𝄞

Root couldn't believe it. Mulch Diggums, one of life's constants. Gone? It couldn't be true.

'He did it too, you know, Foaly. Recovered a copy of the Book no less, and he confirmed Short was alive.'

Foaly's wide brow creased for an instant. 'It's just that ...'

'What?' said Root, suspicion aroused.

'Well, for a moment there, just before the end, his heart rate seemed abnormally fast.'

'Maybe it was a malfunction.'

The centaur was unconvinced. 'I doubt it. My bugs don't have bugs.'

'What other explanation could there be? You still have visuals, don't you?'

'Yep. Through dead eyes, no doubt about it. Not a spark of electricity in that brain; the camera is running on its own battery.'

'Well, that's it then. No other explanation.'

Foaly nodded. 'It would seem that way. Unless ... No, it's too fantastic.'

'This is Mulch Diggums we're talking about here. Nothing is too fantastic.'

Foaly opened his mouth to voice his incredible theory, but before he could speak the shuttle's bay door slid open.

'We have him!' said a triumphant voice.

'Yes!' agreed a second. 'Fowl has made a mistake!'

Root swivelled on his chair. It was Argon and

Cumulus, the so-called behavioural analysts.

'Oh, we've finally decided to earn our retainers, have we?'

But the professors were not so easily intimidated. United by excitement. Cumulus even had the temerity to wave Root's sarcasm aside. This more than anything else made the commander sit up and take notice.

Argon brushed past Foaly, pressing a laser disk into the console's player. Artemis Fowl's face appeared, as seen through Root's iris-cam.

'We'll be in touch,' said the commander's recorded voice. 'Don't worry, I'll see myself out.'

Fowl's face disappeared momentarily as he rose from his chair. Root lifted his gaze in time for the next chilling statement.

'You do that. But remember this, none of your race has permission to enter here while I'm alive.'

Argon pressed the pause button triumphantly. 'There, you see!'

Root's complexion lost any final traces of pallor.

'There? There what? What do I see?'

Cumulus tutted, as one would at a slow child. A mistake, in retrospect. The commander had him by the pointy beard in under a second.

'Now,' he said, his voice deceptively calm. 'Pretend we're pushed for time here and just explain it to me without any attitude or comments.'

'The human said we couldn't enter while he was alive,' squeaked Cumulus.

'So?'

Argon took up the account. 'So ... if we can't go in while he's alive ...'

Root drew a sharp breath. 'Then we go in when he's dead.'

Cumulus and Argon beamed. 'Exactly,' they said in perfect unison.

Root scratched his chin.

'I don't know. We're on shaky ground here legally.'

'Not at all,' argued Cumulus. 'It's elementary grammar. The human specifically stated that entry was forbidden as long as he was alive. That's tantamount to an invitation when he's dead.'

The commander wasn't convinced. 'The invitation is implied, at best.'

'No,' interrupted Foaly. 'They're right. It's a strong case. Once Fowl is dead, the door is wide open. He said it himself.'

'Maybe.'

'Maybe nothing,' blurted Foaly. 'For heaven's sake, Julius, how much more do you need? We have a crisis here, in case you hadn't noticed.'

Root nodded slowly. 'One, you're right. Two, I'm going to run with it. Three, well done, you two. And four, if you ever call me Julius again, Foaly, you'll be eating your own hooves. Now, get me a line to the Council. I need to get approval for that gold.'

'Right away, Commander Root, your worship.' Foaly grinned, letting the hoof-eating comment slide for Holly's sake.

'So we send in the gold,' muttered Root, thinking aloud. 'They send out Holly, we blue-rinse the place and stroll in to reclaim the ransom. Simple.'

'So simple it's brilliant,' enthused Argon. 'Quite a coup for our profession, wouldn't you say, Doctor Cumulus?'

Cumulus's head was spinning with possibilities. 'Lecture tours, book deals. Why, the movie rights alone will be worth a fortune.'

'Let those sociologists stuff this in their collective pipe. Puts the kibosh on the deprivation-breeds-antisocial-behaviour chestnut. This Fowl character has never gone hungry in his life.'

'There's more than one kind of hunger,' noted Argon.

'Very true. Hunger to succeed. Hunger to dominate. Hunger to –'

Root snapped. 'Get out! Get out before I strangle the pair of you. And if I ever hear a word of this repeated on an afternoon talk show, I'll know where it came from.'

The consultants retreated warily, resolving not to call their agents until they were out of earshot.

'I don't know if the Council will go for this,' admitted Root when they'd departed. 'It's a lot of gold.'

Foaly looked up from the console. 'How much exactly?'

The commander slid a piece of paper across the console. 'That much.'

'That is a lot.' Foaly whistled. 'A tonne. Small unmarked ingots. Twenty-four carat only. Well, at least it's a nice round weight.'

'Very comforting. I'll be sure to mention that to the Council. Have you got that line yet?'

The centaur grunted. A negative grunt. Very cheeky really, grunting at a superior officer. Root didn't have the energy to discipline him, but he made a mental note: when this is over, dock Foaly's pay for a few decades. He rubbed his eyes exhaustedly. Time lag was beginning to set in. Even though his brain wouldn't let him sleep because he'd been awake when the time-stop was initiated, his body was crying out for rest.

He rose from the chair, swinging the door wide to let in some air. Stale. Time-stop air. Not even molecules could escape the time-field, much less a human boy.

There was activity by the portal. Lots of it. A swarm of troops gathered around a hovercage. Cudgeon stood at the head of the procession and the entire bunch was heading his way. Root stepped down to meet them.

'What's this?' he inquired, none too pleasantly. 'A circus?'

Cudgeon's face was pale, but determined.

'No, Julius. It's the end of the circus.'

Root nodded. 'I see. And these are the clowns?'

Foaly's head poked through the doorway.

'Pardon me for interrupting your extended circus metaphor, but what the hell is that?'

'Yes, Lieutenant,' said Root, nodding at the floating hovercage. 'What the hell is that?'

Cudgeon bolstered his courage with a few deep breaths. 'I've taken a leaf from your book, Julius.'

'Is that a fact?'

'Yes. It is. You opted to send in a lapsed creature. So now I'm going to.'

Root smiled dangerously. 'You don't opt to do anything, *Lieutenant,* not without my say so.'

Cudgeon took an unconscious step backwards.

'I've been to the Council, Julius. I have their full backing.'

The commander turned to Foaly. 'Is this true?'

'Apparently. It just came through on the outside line. This is Cudgeon's party now. He told the Council about the ransom demand and you springing Mister Diggums. You know what the elders are like when it comes to parting with gold.'

Root folded his arms. 'People told me about you, Cudgeon. They said you'd stab me in the back. I didn't believe them. I was a fool.'

'This is not about us, Julius. It's about the mission.

What's inside this cage is our best chance of success.'

'So what's in the cage? No, don't tell me. The only other non-magical creature in the Lower Elements. And the first troll we've managed to take alive in over a century.'

'Exactly. The perfect creature to flush out our adversary.'

Root's cheeks glowed with the effort of restraining his anger.

'I don't believe you're even considering this.'

'Face it, Julius, it's the same basic idea as yours.'

'No, it isn't. Mulch Diggums made his own choices. He knew the risks.'

'Diggums is dead?'

Root rubbed his eyes again. 'Yes. It would seem so. A cave-in.'

'That just proves I'm right. A troll won't be so easily dispatched.'

'It's a dumb animal, for heaven's sake! How can a troll follow instructions?'

Cudgeon smiled, newborn confidence peeping through his apprehension.

'What instructions? We just point it at the house and get out of the way. I guarantee you those humans will be begging us to come in and rescue them.'

'And what about my officer?'

'We'll have the troll back under lock and key long

before Captain Short is in any danger.'

'You can guarantee that, can you?'

Cudgeon paused. 'That's a chance I'm willing … the Council is willing to take.'

'Politics,' spat Root. 'This is all politics to you, Cudgeon. A nice feather in your cap on the way to a Council seat. You make me sick.'

'Be that as it may, we are proceeding with this strategy. The Council have appointed me Acting Commander, so if you can't put our personal history aside, get the hell out of my way.'

Root stepped aside. 'Don't worry, *Commander*. I don't want anything to do with this butchery. The credit is all yours.'

Cudgeon put on his best sincere face. 'Julius, despite what you think, I have only the interests of the People at heart.'

'One person in particular,' snorted Root.

Cudgeon decided to go for the high moral ground.

'I don't have to stand here listening to this. Every second talking to you is a second wasted.'

Root looked him straight in the eye. 'That's about six hundred years wasted altogether, eh, *friend*?'

Cudgeon didn't answer. What could he say? Ambition had a price, and that price was friendship.

Cudgeon turned to his squad, a group of hand-picked sprites loyal only to him. 'Get the hovercage over to the avenue. We don't green-light until I give the word.'

He brushed past Root, eyes looking anywhere except at his erstwhile friend. Foaly wouldn't let him go without a comment.

'Hey, Cudgeon.'

The Acting Commander couldn't tolerate that tone, not on his first day.

'You watch your mouth, Foaly. No one is indispensable.'

The centaur chuckled. 'Very true. That's the thing about politics, you get one shot.'

Cudgeon was semi-interested in spite of himself.

'I know if it was me,' continued Foaly, 'and I had one chance, just one chance, to book my behind a seat on that Council, I certainly wouldn't entrust my future to a troll.'

And suddenly Cudgeon's new-found confidence evaporated, replaced by a shiny pallor. He wiped his brow, hurrying after the departing hovercage.

'See you tomorrow,' Foaly called after him. 'You'll be taking out my trash.'

Root laughed. Possibly the first time one of Foaly's comments had amused him.

'Good man, Foaly.' He grinned. 'Hit that back-stabber where it hurts, right in the ambition.'

'Thanks, Julius.'

The grin disappeared faster than a deep-fried pit slug in the LEP canteen.

'I've warned you about the Julius thing, Foaly. Now get that outside line open again. I want that gold ready when Cudgeon's plan goes awry. Lobby all my supporters on the Council. I'm pretty sure Lope's one of mine, and Cahartez, possibly Vinyáya. She's always had a thing for me, devilishly attractive as I am.'

'You're joking, of course.'

'I never joke,' said Root, and he said it with a straight face.

Holly had a plan, of sorts. Sneak around shielded, reclaim some fairy weaponry, then cause havoc until Fowl was forced to release her. And if several million Irish pounds' worth of property damage happened to ensue, well, that was just a bonus.

Holly hadn't felt so good in years. Her eyes blazed with power and there were sparks sizzling below every centimetre of skin. She had forgotten just how good running hot felt.

Captain Short felt in control now, on the hunt. This was what she was trained to do. When this affair had started, the advantage had been with the Mud People. But now the boot was on the other foot. She was the hunter and they were the prey.

Holly scaled the great staircase, ever vigilant for the giant manservant. That was one individual she wasn't taking any chances with. If those fingers closed around her skull, she was history, helmet or not, assuming she managed to find a helmet.

The vast house was like a mausoleum – without a single sign of life inside its vaulted rooms. Spooky portraits though. Each one with Fowl eyes, suspicious and glittering. Holly determined to torch the lot of them when she recovered her Neutrino 2000. Vindictive perhaps, but totally justified considering what Artemis Fowl had put her through.

She scaled the steps swiftly, following the curve around to the upper landing. A slot of pale light peeped from under the last door on the corridor. Holly placed her palm against the wood, feeling for vibration. Activity all right. Shouting and footsteps. Thundering this way.

Holly jumped back, flattening herself against the velveteen wallpaper. Not a moment too soon. A hulking shape burst through the doorway and hurtled down the corridor, leaving a maelstrom of air currents in his wake.

'Juliet!' he shouted, his sister's name hanging in the air long after he had disappeared down the stairs.

Don't worry, Butler, thought Holly. She's having the time of her life glued to *Wrestlemania*. But the open door presented a welcome opportunity. She slipped through before the mechanical arm could close it again.

Artemis Fowl was waiting, anti-shield filters cobbled on to his sunglasses.

'Good evening, Captain Short,' he began, confidence

apparently intact. 'At the risk of sounding clichéd, I've been expecting you.'

Holly didn't respond, didn't even look her jailer in the eye. Instead she utilized her training to scan the room, her gaze resting briefly on each surface.

'You are, of course, still bound by the promises made earlier tonight …'

But Holly wasn't listening, she was sprinting towards a stainless-steel workbench bolted to the far wall.

'So, basically, our situation hasn't changed. You are still my hostage.'

'Yeah, yeah, yeah,' muttered Holly, running her fingers over the rows of confiscated Retrieval equipment. She selected a stealth-coated helmet, slipping it over her pointed ears. The pneumatic pads pumped to cradle her crown. She was safe now. Any further commands given by Fowl meant nothing through the reflective visor. A wire mike slotted down automatically. Contact was immediate.

'… on revolving frequencies. Broadcasting on revolving frequencies. Holly, if you can hear me, take cover.'

Holly recognized Foaly's voice. Something familiar in a crazy situation.

'Repeat. Take cover. Cudgeon is sending in a …'

'Something I should know?' said Artemis.

'Quiet,' hissed Holly, worried by the tone of Foaly's usually flippant voice.

'I say again, they are sending in a troll to secure your release.'

Holly started. Cudgeon was calling the shots now. Not good news at all.

Fowl interrupted again.

'It's not polite, you know. Ignoring your host.'

Holly snarled. 'Enough is enough.'

She pulled back her fist, fingers curled in a tight bunch. Artemis didn't flinch. Why would he? Butler always intervened before punches landed. But then something caught his eye, a large figure running down the stairway on the first-floor monitor. It was Butler.

'That's right, rich boy,' said Holly nastily. 'You're on your own this time.'

And before Artemis's eyes had time to widen, Holly put an extra few kilos of spring in her elbow and whacked her abductor right on the nose.

'Oof,' he said, collapsing on to his rear end.

'Oh yes! That felt good.'

Holly focused on the voice buzzing in her ear.

'… we've been feeding a loop to the outside cameras, so the humans won't see anything come up the avenue. But it's on the way, trust me.'

'Foaly. Foaly, come in.'

'Holly? Is that you?'

'The one and only. Foaly, there is no loop. I can see everything that's going on around here.'

'The cunning little ... He must have rebooted the system.'

The avenue was a hive of fairy activity. Cudgeon was there, haughtily directing his team of sprites. And in the centre of the melee stood a five-metre-tall hovercage, floating on a cushion of air. The cage was directly before the manor door, and the techies were securing a concussor seal to the surrounding wall. When activated, several alloy rods in the seal's collar would be detonated simultaneously, effectively disintegrating the door. When the dust settled, the troll would have only one place to go — into the manor.

Holly checked the other monitors. Butler had managed to drag Juliet from the cell. They had ascended from the cellar level and were just crossing the lobby. Right in the line of fire.

'D'Arvit,' she swore, crossing to the work surface.

Artemis was propped on his elbows. 'You hit me,' he said in disbelief.

Holly strapped on a set of Hummingbirds.

'That's right, Fowl. And there's plenty more where that came from. So stay right where you are, if you know what's good for you.'

For once in his life, Artemis realized that he didn't have a snappy answer. He opened his mouth, waiting for his brain to supply the customary pithy comeback. But nothing arrived.

Holly slipped the Neutrino 2000 into its holster.

'That's right, Mud Boy. Playtime's over. Time for the professionals to take over. If you're a good boy I'll buy you a lolly when I come back.'

And when Holly was long gone, soaring beneath the hallway's ancient oak beams, Artemis said, 'I don't like lollipops.'

It was a woefully inadequate response, and Artemis was instantly appalled with himself. Pathetic really: I don't like lollipops. No self-respecting criminal mastermind would be caught dead even using the word lollipops. He really would have to put together a database of witty responses for occasions such as this.

It was quite possible that Artemis would have sat like that for some time, totally detached from the situation at hand, had not the front door imploded, shaking the manor to its foundations. A thing like that is enough to knock the daydreams from anyone's head.

A sprite alighted before Acting Commander Cudgeon.

'The collar is in place, sir.'

Cudgeon nodded. 'Are you sure it's tight, Captain? I don't want that troll coming out the wrong way.'

'Tighter 'n a goblin's wallet. There's not a bubble of air getting through that seal. Tighter 'n a stink-worm's —'

'Very well, Captain,' interrupted Cudgeon hurriedly, before the sprite could complete his graphic analogy.

Beside them the hovercage shook violently, almost toppling the container from its air cushion.

'We better blow that sucker, Commander. If we don't let him outta there soon, my boys're gonna spend the next week scraping ...'

'Fine, Captain, fine. Blow it. Blow it for goodness' sake.'

Cudgeon hurried behind the blast shield, scribbling a note on his palmtop's LCD screen. Memo: Remind the sprites to watch their language. After all, I am a *Commander* now.

The foul-mouthed captain in question turned to the hovercage's cab driver.

'Blow 'er, Chix. Blow the door off its damn hinges.'

'Yessir. Off its damn hinges. That's a roger.'

Cudgeon winced. There'd be a general meeting tomorrow. First thing. By then he'd have the commander's icon on his lapel. Even a sprite might be less likely to curse, with the triple acorn logo winking in his face.

Chix pulled down his shrapnel goggles, even though the cab had a quartz windscreen. The goggles were cool. Girls loved them. Or so the driver thought. In his mind's eye he saw himself as a grim-faced daredevil. Sprites were like that. Give a fairy a pair of wings and he thinks he's God's gift to women. But Chix Verbil's ill-fated quest to impress the dames is, once again, another story. In this particular tale, he serves only one purpose. And that is to melodramatically push the detonate button. Which he does, with great aplomb.

Two dozen controlled charges detonated in their chambers, driving two dozen alloy cylinders out of their mounts at over a thousand miles per hour. Upon impact, each bar pulverized the contact area plus the surrounding fifteen centimetres, effectively blowing the door off its damn hinges. As the captain would say.

When the dust settled, the handlers winched back the containment wall inside the cage and began hammering the side panels with the flats of their hands.

Cudgeon peeped out from behind the blast shield.

'All clear, Captain?'

'Just a damn second, Commander. Chix? How're we doin'?'

Chix checked the cab's monitor.

'He's movin'. The hammerin' is spookin' him. The claws are comin' out. My, he's a big sucker. I wouldn't wanna be that Recon babe if she gets in the way of this.'

Cudgeon felt a momentary pang of guilt, which he dispelled with his favourite daydream – a vision of himself sinking into a beige-velour Council seat.

The cage heaved violently, almost dislodging Chix from his seat. He held on like a rodeo rider.

'Woah! He's on the move. Lock and load, boys. I have a feeling that any second we're going to be gettin' a cry for help.'

🐚 ✡ 🐑 ◗ ✴ • 🐑 • 🐚 🐑 ◗ • ◗ 🐚 🐚 ○ 🐚 •

Cudgeon didn't bother locking and loading. He preferred to leave that sort of thing to the foot soldiers. The Acting Commander considered himself too important to be risked in an insecure situation. For the good of the People in general, it was better he remain outside the op zone.

Butler took the stairs four at a time. It was possibly the first time he had ever abandoned Master Artemis in a crisis. But Juliet was family, and there was obviously something seriously wrong with his baby sister. That fairy had said something to her and now she was just sitting in the cell giggling. Butler feared the worst. If anything were to happen to Juliet, he didn't know how he'd live with himself.

He felt a dribble of sweat slide down the crown of his shaven head. This whole situation was shooting off in bizarre directions. Fairies, magic, and now a hostage loose in the manor. How could he be expected to control things? It took a four-man team to guard the lowliest politician, but he was expected to contain this impossible situation on his own.

Butler sprinted down the corridor into what had until recently been Captain Short's cell. Juliet was sprawled on the cot, enraptured by a concrete wall.

'What are you doing?' he gasped, drawing the Sig Sauer nine-millimetre with practised ease.

His sister barely spared him a glance. 'Quiet, you big ape. Louie the Love Machine is on. He ain't so tough, I could take him.'

Butler blinked. She was talking gibberish. Obviously drugged.

'Let's go. Artemis wants us upstairs in the situations room.'

Juliet pointed a manicured finger at the wall.

'Artemis can wait. This is for the intercontinental title. And it's a grudge match. Louie ate the Hogman's pet piggie.'

The manservant studied the wall. It was definitely blank. He didn't have time for this.

'Right. Let's go,' he growled, slinging his sister over a broad shoulder.

'Nooo. You big bully,' she protested, hammering his back with tiny fists. 'Not now. Hogman! Hogmaaaan!'

Butler ignored the objections, settling into a loping run. Who the hell was this Hogman person? One of her boyfriends no doubt. He was going to keep closer tabs on callers to the lodge in future.

'Butler? Pick up.'

It was Artemis, on the hand-held. Butler jiggled his sister up a foot so he could reach his belt.

'Lollipops!' barked his employer.

'Say again. I thought you said –'

'Eh ... I mean get out of there. Take cover! Take cover!'

Take cover? The military term didn't sound right coming out of Master Artemis's mouth. Like a diamond ring in a Lucky Bag.

'Take cover?'

'Yes, Butler. Cover. I thought speaking in primal terms would be the quickest route to your cognitive functions. Obviously I was mistaken.'

That was more like it. Butler scanned the hall for a nook to duck into. Not much choice. The only shelter was provided by the suits of medieval armour punctuating the walls. The manservant ducked into the alcove behind a fourteenth-century knight complete with lance and mace.

Juliet tapped the breastplate.

'You think you're mean? I could take you with one hand.'

'Quiet,' hissed Butler.

He held his breath and listened. Something was approaching the main door. Something big. Butler leaned out far enough to get one eye on the lobby …

Then you could say that the doorway exploded. But that particular verb doesn't do the action justice. Rather, it shattered into infinitesimal pieces. Butler had seen something like this once before when a force-seven earthquake had rippled through a Colombian drug lord's estate seconds before he had been scheduled to blow it up. This was slightly different. More localized. Very professional. It was classic anti-terrorist tactics. Hit 'em with smoke and sonics, then go in while the targets were disoriented. Whatever was coming, it would be bad. He was certain of it. He was absolutely right.

Dust clouds settled slowly, depositing a pale sheet on the Tunisian rug. Madam Fowl would have been furious, if she ever put so much as a toe outside the attic door. Butler's instincts told him to move. Zigzag across the ground floor, make for the higher ground. Stay low to minimize the target. This would be the perfect time to do it, before visibility cleared. Any second now, a hail of bullets would be whistling through the archway, and the last place he wanted to be was pinned down on a lower level.

And on any other day Butler would have moved. He would've been halfway up that stairway before his brain had time for second thoughts. But today he had his baby sister over his shoulder spouting gibberish, and the last thing he wanted to do was expose her to murderous assault fire. With Juliet in the state she was in, she'd probably challenge the fairy commandos to a tag-wrestling match. And though his sister talked tough, she was just a kid really. No match for trained military personnel. So Butler hunkered down, propped Juliet against a tapestry behind a suit of armour and checked his safety catch. Off. Good. Come and get me, fairy boys.

Something moved in the dust haze. It was immediately obvious to Butler that the *something* wasn't human. The manservant had been on too many safaris not to recognize an animal when he saw it. He studied the creature's gait. Possibly simian. Similar upper-body structure to an ape, but bigger than any primate Butler had ever seen. If it was an ape, then his handgun wasn't going to be of much use. You could put five rounds in the skull of a bull ape and he'd still have time to eat you before his brain realized he was dead.

But it wasn't an ape. Apes didn't have night eyes. This creature did. Glowing crimson pupils, half-hidden behind shaggy forelocks. Tusks too, but not elephantine. These were curved, with serrated edges. Gutting weapons. Butler felt a tingle low in his stomach. He'd had the feeling once before. On his first day at the Swiss academy. It was fear.

The creature stepped clear of the dust haze. Butler gasped. Again, his first since the academy. This was like no adversary he'd ever faced before. The manservant realized instantly what the fairies had done. They had sent in a primal hunter. A creature with no interest in magic or rules. A thing that would simply kill anything in its way, regardless of species. This was the perfect predator. That much was clear from the meat-ripping points on its teeth, from the dried gore crusted beneath its claws and from the distilled hatred spilling from its eyes.

The troll shambled forwards, squinting through the chandelier light. Yellowed claws scraped along the marble tiling, throwing up sparks in their wake. It was sniffing now, snorting curious breaths, head cocked to one side. Butler had seen that pose before — on the snouts of starved pit bulls, just before their Russian handlers set them loose on a bear hunt.

The shaggy head froze, its snout pointed directly at Butler's hiding place. It was no coincidence. The manservant peeked out between the chain-mail fingers of a gauntlet. Now came the stalk. Once a scent had been acquired, the predator would attempt a slow silent approach, before the lightning strike.

But apparently the troll had not read the predator's handbook, because it didn't bother with the stealth approach, jumping directly to the lightning strike. Moving faster than Butler would have believed possible, the troll sprang across the lobby, brushing the medieval armour aside as though it were a shop mannequin.

Juliet blinked. 'Ooh,' she gasped. 'It's Bigfoot Bob. Canadian champion nineteen ninety-eight. I thought you were in the Andes, looking for your relatives.'

Butler didn't bother to correct her. His sister wasn't lucid. At least she would die happy. While his brain was contemplating this morbid observation, Butler's gun hand was coming up.

He squeezed the trigger as rapidly as the Sig Sauer's mechanism would allow. Two in the chest, three between the eyes. That was the plan. He got the chest shots in, but the troll interfered before Butler could complete the formation. The interference took the form of scything tusks that ducked below Butler's guard. They coiled around his trunk, slicing through his Kevlar reinforced jacket like a razor through rice paper.

Butler felt a cold pain as the serrated ivory pierced his chest. He knew immediately that the wound was fatal. His breath came hard. That was a lung gone, and gouts of blood were matting the troll's fur. His blood. No one could lose that amount and live. Nevertheless, the pain was instantly replaced by a curious euphoria. Some form of natural anaesthetic injected through channels in the beast's tusks. More dangerous than the deadliest poison. In minutes Butler would not only stop struggling, but go giggling to his grave.

The manservant fought against the narcotics in his system, struggling furiously in the troll's grip. But it was no use. His fight was over almost before it had begun.

The troll grunted, flipping the limp human body over his head. Butler's burly frame collided with the wall at a speed human bones were never meant to withstand. The bricks cracked from floor to ceiling. Butler's spine went too. Now, even if the blood loss didn't get him, paralysis would.

Juliet was still enthralled by the *mesmer*.

'Come on, brother. Get off the canvas. We all know you're faking.'

The troll paused, some basic curiosity piqued by the lack of fear. He would have suspected a trick, if he could have formulated such a complicated thought. But in the end, appetite won out. This creature smelled flesh. Fresh and tender. Flesh from above ground was different. Laced with surface smells. Once you've had open-air meat, it's hard to go back. The troll ran a tongue over his incisors and reached out a shaggy hand ...

Holly tucked the Hummingbirds close to her torso, dropping into a controlled dive. She skimmed the banisters, emerging into the portico below a stained-glass dome. The time-stop light filtered unnaturally, splitting into thick azure shafts.

Light, thought Holly. The helmet high-beams worked before, there was no reason why they wouldn't work again. It was too late for the male, he was a bag of broken bones. But the female, she still had a few seconds left before the troll split her open.

Holly spiralled down through the *faux* light, searching her helmet console for the Sonix button. Sonix were generally used on canines, but in this case it might provide a moment's distraction. Enough to get her to ground level.

The troll was reaching in towards Juliet underhand. It was a move generally reserved for the defenceless. The claws would curl in below the ribs, rupturing the heart.

Minimum damage to the flesh and no last-minute tension to toughen the meat.

Holly activated her Sonix ... and nothing happened. Not good. Generally your average troll would be at the very least irritated by the ultra-high-frequency tone. But this particular beast didn't even shake his shaggy head. There were a couple of possibilities: one, the helmet was malfunctioning; two, this troll was deaf as the proverbial post. Unfortunately, Holly had no way of knowing as the tones were inaudible to fairy ears.

Whatever the problem, it forced Holly to adopt a strategy she would rather not have resorted to. Direct contact. All to save a human's life. She'd gone section eight. Without a doubt.

Holly jerked the throttle, straight from fourth to reverse. Not very good for the gears. She'd get a dressing-down from the mechanics for that, in the unlikely event she actually survived this never-ending nightmare. The effect of this gear-crunching was to flip her around in mid-air, so that her boot heels were pointed directly at the troll's head. Holly winced. Two entanglements with the same troll. Unbelievable.

Her heels caught the beast square on the crown of its head. At that speed, there was at least half a tonne of G-force behind the contact. Only the reinforced ribbing in her suit prevented Holly's leg bones from shattering. Even so, she heard her knee pop. The pain clawed its way to her forehead. Ruined her recovery manoeuvre too. Instead of repelling herself to a safe altitude, Holly crumpled on to the troll's back, becoming instantly entangled in the ropy fur.

The troll was suitably annoyed. Not only had something distracted it from dinner, but now that something was nestled in its fur, along with the cleaner slugs. The beast straightened, reaching a clawed hand over its own shoulder. The curved nails raked Holly's helmet, scoring parallel grooves in the alloy. Juliet was safe for the moment, but Holly had taken her place on the endangered-individuals list.

The troll squeezed tighter, somehow securing a grip on the helmet's anti-friction coating, which, according to Foaly, was impossible to grip. Serious words would be had. If not in this life, then definitely the next.

Captain Short found herself being hoisted aloft to face her old enemy. Holly struggled to concentrate through the pain and confusion. Her leg was swinging like a pendulum, and the troll's breath was breaking over her face in rancid waves.

There had been a plan, hadn't there? Surely she didn't fly down here just to curl up and die. There must have been a strategy. All those years in the Academy must have taught her something. Whatever her plan had been, it floated just out of reach somewhere between pain and shock. Out of reach.

'The lights, Holly ...'

A voice in her head. Probably talking to herself. An out-of-head experience. Ha ha. She must remember to tell Foaly about this ... Foaly?

'Hit the lights, Holly. If those tusks get to work, you'll be dead before the magic can kick in.'

'Foaly? Is that you?' Holly may have said this aloud, or she may just have thought it. She wasn't sure.

'The tunnel high beams, Captain!' A different voice. Not so cuddly. 'Hit the button now! That's an order!'

Oops. It was Root. She was falling down on the job again. First Hamburg, then Martina Franca, now this.

'Yessir,' she mumbled, trying to sound professional.

'Press it! Now, Captain Short!'

Holly looked the troll straight in its merciless eyes and pressed the button. Very melodramatic. Or it would have been, if the lights had worked. Unfortunately for Holly, in her haste she'd grabbed one of the helmets cannibalized by Artemis Fowl. Hence no Sonix, no filters and no tunnel beams. The halogen bulbs were still installed, but the wires had come loose during Artemis's investigations.

'Oh dear,' breathed Holly.

'Oh dear!' barked Root. 'What's that supposed to mean?'

'The beams are off-line,' explained Foaly.

'Oh ...' Root's voice trailed off. What more was there to say?

Holly squinted at the troll. If you didn't know trolls were dumb animals, you'd swear the beast was grinning. Standing there with blood dripping from various chest wounds, grinning. Captain Short didn't like being grinned at.

'Laugh this off,' she said, and butted the troll with the only weapon available to her. Her helmeted head.

Valiant undoubtedly, but about as effective as trying to cut down a tree with a feather. Luckily, the ill-advised blow had a side effect. For a split second, two strands of conductor filament connected, sending power flooding to one of the tunnel beams. Four-hundred watts of white light blasted through the troll's crimson eyes, dispatching lightning rods of agony to the brain.

'Heh heh,' mumbled Holly, in the second before the troll convulsed involuntarily. Its spasms sent her spinning across the parquet floor, leg jittering along behind her.

The wall was approaching at an alarming speed. Maybe, thought Holly hopefully, this will be one of those impacts where you don't feel any pain until later. No, replied her pessimistic side, afraid not. She slammed into a Norman narrative tapestry, bringing it tumbling down on top of her. Pain was immediate and overwhelming.

'Ooof,' grunted Foaly. 'I felt that. Visuals are shot. Pain sensors went right off the scale. Your lungs are busted, Captain. We're going to lose you for a while. But don't worry, Holly, your magic should be kicking in already.'

232

Holly felt the blue tingle of magic scurrying to her various injuries. Thank the gods for acorns. But it was too little too late. The pain was way beyond her threshold. Just before unconsciousness claimed her, Holly's hand flopped from beneath the tapestry. It landed on Butler's arm, touching the bare skin. Amazingly, the human wasn't dead. A dogged pulse forced the blood through smashed limbs.

Heal, thought Holly. And the magic scurried down her fingers.

The troll faced a dilemma – which female to eat first. Choices, choices. This decision was not made any easier by the lingering agony buzzing around its shaggy head, or the cluster of bullets lodged in the fatty chest tissue. Eventually it settled on the surface dweller. Soft human meat. No dense fairy muscle to chew through.

The beast squatted low, tilting the girl's chin with one yellowed talon. A pulsing jugular looped lazily down the length of her neck. The heart or the neck? the troll wondered. The neck, it was closer. It turned the talon sideways, so that the edge pressed against soft human flesh. One sharp swipe and the girl's own heartbeat would drive the blood from her body.

Butler woke up, which was a surprise in itself. He knew immediately that he was alive, because of the searing pain permeating every cubic centimetre of his body. This was not good. Alive he may have been, but considering the fact that his neck had a one-eighty twist on it, he'd never so much as walk the dog again, not to mention rescue his sister.

The manservant twiddled his fingers. Hurt like hell, but at least there was movement. It was amazing that he had any motor functions at all, considering the trauma his spinal column had suffered. His toes seemed all right too, but that could have been phantom response, given that he couldn't actually see them.

The bleeding from his chest wound appeared to have stopped and he was thinking straight. All in all, he was in much better shape than he had any right to be. What in heaven's name was going on here?

Butler noticed something. There were blue sparks dancing along his torso. He must be hallucinating, creating pleasant images to distract himself from the inevitable. A very realistic hallucination, it must be said.

The sparks congregated at trauma points, sinking into the skin. Butler shuddered. This was no hallucination. Something extraordinary was happening here. Magical.

Magic? That rang a bell in his recently reassembled cranium. Fairy magic. Something was healing his wounds. He twisted his head, wincing at the grate of sliding vertebrae. There was a hand resting on his forearm. Sparks flowed from the slim elfin fingers, intuitively targeting bruises, breaks or ruptures. There were a lot of injuries to be dealt with, but the tiny sparks handled it all quickly and effectively. Like an army of mystical beavers repairing storm damage.

Butler could actually feel his bones knitting and the blood retreating from semi-congealed scabs. His head twisted involuntarily as his vertebrae slid into their niches, and strength returned in a rush as magic reproduced the three litres of blood lost through his chest wound.

Butler jumped to his feet – actually jumped. He was himself again. No. It was more than that. He was as strong as he had ever been. Strong enough to have another crack at that beast hunkered over his baby sister.

He felt his rejuvenated heart speed up like the stroke of an outboard motor. Calm, Butler told himself. Passion is the enemy of efficiency. But calm or no, the situation was desperate. This beast had already effectively killed him once, and this time round he didn't even have the Sig Sauer. His own skills aside, it would be nice to have a weapon. Something with a bit of weight to it. His boot clinked on a metallic object. Butler glanced down at the debris strewn in the troll's wake ... Perfect.

There was nothing but snow on the viewscreen.

'Come on,' urged Root. 'Hurry up!'

Foaly elbowed past his superior.

'Maybe if you didn't insist on blocking all the circuit boards.'

Root shuffled out of the way grudgingly. In his mind it was the circuit boards' fault for being behind him. The centaur's head disappeared into an access panel.

'Anything?'

'Nothing. Just interference.'

Root slapped the screen. Not a good idea. First, because there was not one chance in a million that it would actually help, and second, because plasma screens grow extremely hot after prolonged use.

'D'Arvit!'

'Don't touch that screen, by the way.'

'Oh, ha ha. We have time for jokes now, do we?'

'No, actually. Anything?'

The snow settled into recognizable shapes.

'That's it, hold it there. We've got a signal.'

'I've activated the secondary camera. Plain old video, I'm afraid, but it'll have to do.'

Root didn't comment. He was watching the screen. This must be a movie. It couldn't be real life.

'So what's going on in there? Anything interesting?'

Root tried to answer, but his soldier's vocabulary just didn't have the superlatives.

'What? What is it?'

The commander made an attempt. 'It's … the human

… I've never … Oh, forget it, Foaly. You're going to have to see this for yourself.'

Holly watched the entire episode through a gap in the tapestry folds. If she hadn't seen it, she wouldn't have believed it. In fact, it wasn't until she'd reviewed the VT for her report that she was certain the whole thing wasn't a hallucination brought on by a near-death experience. As it was, the video sequence became something of a legend, iinitially doing the rounds on the *Amateur Home Movies* cable shows and ending up on the LEP Academy Hand-to-hand curriculum.

The human, Butler, was strapping on a medieval suit of armour. Incredible as it seemed, he apparently intended going toe to toe with the troll. Holly tried to warn him, tried to make some sound, but the magic hadn't yet reinflated her crushed lungs.

Butler closed his visor, hefting a vicious mace.

'Now,' he grunted through the grille. 'I'll show you what happens when someone lays a hand on my sister.'

The human twirled the mace as though it were a cheerleader's baton, ramming it home between the troll's shoulder blades. A blow like that, while not fatal, certainly distracted the troll from its intended victim.

Butler planted his foot just above the creature's haunches and tugged the weapon free. It relinquished its grip with a sickly sucking sound. He skipped backwards, settling into a defensive stance.

The troll rounded on him, all ten talons sliding out to their full extent. Drops of venom glistened from the tip of each tusk. Playtime was over. But there would be no lightning strike this time. The beast was wary, it had been hurt. This latest attacker would be afforded the same respect as another male of the species. As far as the troll was concerned, his territory was being encroached on. And there was only one way of solving a dispute of this nature. The same way that trolls solved every dispute ...

'I must warn you,' said Butler, straight-faced. 'I am armed and prepared to use deadly force if necessary.'

Holly would have groaned if she could. Banter! The human was trying to engage a troll in macho repartee! Then Captain Short realized her mistake. The words weren't important, it was the tone he employed. Calm, soothing. Like a trainer with a spooked unicorn.

'Step away from the female. Easy now.'

The troll ballooned its cheeks and howled. Scare tactics. Testing the waters. Butler didn't flinch.

'Yeah, yeah. Real scary. Now just back out of the door, and I won't have to cut you into little pieces.'

The troll snorted, miffed by this reaction. Generally his roar sent whatever creature was facing it scurrying down the tunnel.

'One step at a time. Nice and slow. Easy there, big fellow.'

You could almost see it in the troll's eyes. A flicker of uncertainty. Maybe this human was ...

And that was when Butler struck. He danced under the tusks, hammering home a devastating uppercut with his medieval weapon. The troll staggered backwards, talons flailing wildly. But it was too late: Butler had stepped out of reach, scooting across to the other side of the corridor.

The troll lumbered after him, spitting dislodged teeth from pulped gums. Butler sank to his knees, sliding and turning, the polished floor bearing him like an ice skater. He ducked and pirouetted, facing his pursuer.

'Guess what I found?' he said, raising the Sig Sauer.

No chest shots this time. Butler laid in the rest of the automatic's clip in a ten-centimetre diameter between the troll's eyes. Unfortunately for Butler, due to millennia spent butting each other, trolls have developed a thick ridge of bone covering their brows. So his textbook spread failed to penetrate the skull, in spite of the Teflon-coated load.

However, ten Devastator slugs can't be ignored by any creature on the planet, and the troll was no exception. The bullets beat a sledgehammer tattoo on its cranium causing instant concussion. The animal staggered backwards, slapping at its own forehead. Butler was after it in a heartbeat, pinning one shaggy foot beneath the mace spikes.

The troll was concussed, blinded by blood, and lame.

A normal person would feel a shard of remorse, but not Butler. He'd seen too many men gored by injured animals. Now was the dangerous time. It was no time for mercy, it was time to terminate with extreme prejudice.

Holly could only watch helplessly as the human took careful aim and delivered a series of crippling blows to the stricken creature. First he took out the tendons, bringing the troll to its knees, then he abandoned the mace and went to work with gauntleted hands, perhaps deadlier than the mace had been. The unfortunate troll fought back pathetically, even managing to land a few glancing blows. But they failed to penetrate the antique armour. Meanwhile Butler toiled like a surgeon. Working on the assumption that the troll and human physiques were basically the same, he rained blow after blow on the dumb creature, reducing it to a heap of quivering fur in so many seconds. It was pitiful to watch. And the manservant wasn't finished yet. He stripped off the bloodied gauntlets, loading a fresh clip into the handgun.

'Let's see how much bone you have under your chin.'

'No,' gasped Holly, with the first breath in her body. 'Don't.'

Butler ignored her, jamming the barrel beneath the troll's jaw.

'Don't do it …You owe me.'

Butler paused. Juliet was alive, it was true. Confused certainly, but alive. He thumbed the hammer on his pistol. Every brain cell in his head screamed for him to pull the trigger. But Juliet was alive.

'You owe me, human.'

Butler sighed. He'd regret this later.

'Very well, Captain. The beast lives to fight another day. Lucky for him, I'm in a good mood.'

Holly made a noise. It was somewhere between a whimper and a chuckle.

'Now let's get rid of our hairy friend.'

Butler rolled the unconscious troll on to an armour trolley, dragging it to the devastated doorway. With a huge heave, he jettisoned the lot into the suspended night.

'And don't come back,' he shouted.

'Amazing,' said Root.

'Tell me about it,' agreed Foaly.

CHAPTER 9: ACE IN THE HOLE

 ARTEMIS tried the doorknob and got a scorched palm for his trouble. Sealed. The fairy must have blasted it with her weapon. Very astute. One less variable in the equation. It was exactly what he himself would have done.

Artemis did not waste any time attempting to force open the door. It was reinforced steel and he was twelve. You didn't have to be a genius to figure it out, even though he was. Instead the Fowl heir apparent crossed to the monitor wall and followed developments from there.

He knew immediately what the LEP were up to – send in the troll to secure a cry for help, interpret it as an invitation, and next thing you know a brigade of goblin stormtroopers were taking the manor. Clever. And unanticipated. It was the second time he'd underestimated his opponents. One way or another, there wouldn't be a third.

As the drama below unfolded on the monitors, Artemis's emotions jumped from terror to pride. Butler had done it. Defeated the troll, and without a single plea for aid passing his lips. Watching the display, Artemis appreciated fully, perhaps for the first time, the service provided by the Butler family.

Artemis activated the tri-band radio, broadcasting on revolving frequencies.

'Commander Root, you are monitoring all channels I presume ...'

For a few moments nothing but white noise emanated from the micro speakers, then Artemis heard the sharp click of a mike button.

'I hear you, human. What can I do for you?'

'Is that the commander?'

A noise filtered through the black gauze. It sounded like a whinny.

'No. This is not the commander. This is Foaly, the centaur. Is that the kidnapping lowlife human?'

It took Artemis a moment to process the fact that he'd been insulted.

'Mister ... ah ... Foaly. You have obviously not studied your psych texts. It is not wise to antagonize the hostage-taker. I may be unstable.'

'*May* be unstable? There's no *may* about it. Not that it

matters. Soon you'll be no more than a cloud of radioactive molecules.'

Artemis chuckled. 'That's where you are mistaken, my quadrupedal friend. By the time that bio-bomb is detonated, I will be long gone from this time-stop.'

It was Foaly's turn to chuckle. 'You're bluffing, human. If there was a way to escape the field, I would have found it. I think you're talking through your –'

Thankfully it was at that moment Root took over at the microphone.

'Fowl? This is Commander Root. What do you want?'

'I would just like to inform you, Commander, that in spite of your attempted betrayal, I am still willing to negotiate.'

'That troll had nothing to do with me,' protested Root. 'It was done against my wishes.'

'The fact is that it *was* done, and by the LEP. Whatever trust we had is gone. So here is my ultimatum. You have thirty minutes to send in the gold, or else I will refuse to release Captain Short. Furthermore, I will not take her with me when I leave the time-field, leaving her to be disintegrated by the bio-bomb.'

'Don't be a fool, human. You're deluding yourself. Mud technology is aeons behind ours. There is *no way* to escape the time-field.'

Artemis leaned in close to the mike, smiling his wolfish smile.

'There's only one way to find out, Root. Are you willing to bet Captain Short's life on your hunch?'

Root's hesitation was highlighted by the hiss of interference. His reply, when it came, was tinged with just the right note of defeat.

'No,' he sighed. 'I'm not. You'll have your gold, Fowl. A tonne. Twenty-four carat.'

Artemis smirked. Quite the actor, our Commander Root.

'Thirty minutes, Commander. Count the seconds if your clock's stopped. I'm waiting. But not for long.'

Artemis terminated the contact, settling back in the swivel chair. It would seem as though the bait had been taken. No doubt the LEP analysts had discovered his 'accidental' invitation. The fairies would pay up because they believed the gold would be theirs again as soon as he was dead. Vaporized by the bio-bomb. Which, of course, he wouldn't be. In theory.

Butler put three rounds into the door frame. The door itself was steel and would have sent the Devastator slugs ricocheting straight back at him. But the frame was the original porous stone used to build the manor. It crumbled like chalk. A very basic security flaw, and one that would have to be remedied once this business was over.

Master Artemis was waiting calmly in his chair by the monitor bank.

'Nice work, Butler.'

'Thank you, Artemis. We were in trouble for a moment there. If it hadn't been for the captain …'

Artemis nodded. 'Yes. I saw. Healing, one of the fairy arts. I wonder why she did it.'

'I wonder too,' said Butler softly. 'We certainly didn't deserve it.'

Artemis glanced up sharply. 'Keep the faith, old friend. The end is in sight.'

Butler nodded; he even attempted a smile. But though there were plenty of teeth in the grin, there was no heart.

'In less than an hour, Captain Short will be back with her people and we will have sufficient funds to relaunch some of our more tasteful enterprises.'

'I know. It's just …'

Artemis didn't have to ask. He knew exactly what Butler was feeling. The fairy had saved both their lives and yet he insisted on holding her to ransom. To a man of honour like Butler, this was almost more than he could bear.

'The negotiations are over. One way or another she will be returned to her kind. No harm will befall Captain Short. You have my word.'

'And Juliet?'

'Yes?'

'Is there any danger to my sister?'

'No. No danger.'

'The fairies are just going to give us this gold and walk away?'

Artemis snorted gently. 'No, not exactly. They're going to bio-bomb Fowl Manor the second Captain Short is clear.'

Butler took a breath to speak, but hesitated. Obviously there was more to the plan. Master Fowl would tell him when he needed to know. So instead of quizzing his employer, he made a simple statement.

'I trust you, Artemis.'

'Yes,' replied the boy, the weight of that trust etched on his brow. 'I know.'

Cudgeon was doing what politicians did best: trying to duck responsibility.

'Your officer helped the humans,' he blurted, mustering as much indignation as possible. 'The entire operation was proceeding exactly as planned, until your female attacked our deputy.'

'Deputy?' chortled Foaly. 'Now the troll's a deputy.'

'Yes. He is. And that human made mincemeat of him. This entire situation could be wrapped up if it wasn't for your department's incompetence.'

Ordinarily, Root would have blown his top at this point, but he knew that Cudgeon was grasping at straws, desperately trying to save his career. So the commander just smiled.

'Hey, Foaly?'

'Yes, Commander?'

'Did we get the troll assault on disk?'

The centaur heaved a dramatic sigh. 'No, sir, we ran out of disks just before the troll went in.'

'What a pity.'

'A real shame.'

'Those disks could have been invaluable to Acting Commander Cudgeon at his hearing.'

Cudgeon's cool went out the window. 'Give me those disks, Julius! I know they're in there! This is blatant obstruction.'

'You're the only one guilty of obstruction around here, Cudgeon. Using this affair to further your own career.'

Cudgeon's face took on a hue to match Root's own. The situation was slipping away from him and he knew it. Even Chix Verbil and the other sprites were sidling out from behind their leader.

'I am still in charge here, Julius, so hand over those disks or I *will* have you detained.'

'Oh, really? You and whose army?'

For a second Cudgeon's face glowed with the old pomposity. It evaporated the moment he noticed the conspicuous lack of officers at his shoulders.

'That's right,' snickered Foaly. 'You ain't Acting Commander any more. The call came through from below. You've got an appointment with the Council, and I don't think it's to offer you a seat.'

It was probably Foaly's grin that drove Cudgeon over the edge.

'Give me those disks!' he roared, pinning Foaly to the operation's shuttle.

Root was tempted to let them wrestle for a while, but now wasn't the time to indulge himself.

'Naughty naughty,' he said, pointing his index finger at Cudgeon. 'No one beats Foaly but me.'

Foaly paled. 'Careful with that finger. You're still wearing the —'

Root's thumb *accidentally* brushed his knuckle, opening a tiny gas valve. The released gas propelled a tranquillized dart through the latex fingertip and straight into Cudgeon's neck. The Acting Commander, soon to be Private, sank like a stone.

Foaly rubbed his neck. 'Nice shot, Commander.'

'I don't know what you're talking about. Total accident. I forgot all about the fake finger. There are several precedents, I believe.'

'Oh, absolutely. Unfortunately Cudgeon will be unconscious for several hours. By the time he awakens, all the excitement will be over.'

'Shame.' Root allowed himself a fleeting grin, then it was back to business. 'Is the gold here?'

'Yep, they just inserted it.'

'Good.' He called to Cudgeon's sheepish troops. 'Get

it loaded on a hovertrolley and send it in. Any trouble and I'll feed you your wings. Understood?'

No one actually replied, but it was understood. No doubt about it.

'Good. Now hop to it.'

Root disappeared into the operation's shuttle, Foaly clopping behind him. The commander shut the door firmly.

'Is it armed?'

The centaur flicked a few important-looking switches on the main console.

'It is now.'

'I want it launched as soon as possible.' He glanced through the laser-proof refractor glass. 'We're down to minutes here. I see sunlight poking through.'

Foaly bent to his keyboard in earnest. 'The magic is breaking up. In fifteen minutes we're going to be in the middle of overground daytime. The neutrino streams are losing their integrity.'

'I see,' said Root, which was basically a lie again. 'OK, I don't see. But I do get the fifteen minutes bit. That gives you ten minutes to get Captain Short out of there. After that we're going to be sitting ducks for the entire human race.'

Foaly activated yet another camera. This one was linked to the hovertrolley. He ran a finger experimentally across a trackpad. The trolley shot forward, almost decapitating Chix Verbil.

'Nice driving,' muttered Root. 'Will it get up the steps?'

Foaly didn't even look up from his computers.

'Automatic clearance compensator. One-point-five metre collar. No problems.'

Root speared him with a glare. 'You do that just to annoy me, don't you?'

Foaly shrugged his shoulders. 'I might do.'

'Yes, well, count yourself lucky my other fingers aren't loaded. Get my meaning?'

'Yessir.'

'Good. Now let's bring Captain Short home.'

Holly hovered beneath the portico. Orange shards of light striped the blue. The time-stop was breaking up. There were only minutes left before Root blue-rinsed the whole place. Foaly's voice buzzed in her earpiece.

'OK, Captain Short. The gold is on the way. Be ready to move.'

'We don't bargain with kidnappers,' said Holly, surprised. 'What's going on here?'

'Nothing,' replied Foaly casually. 'Straightforward exchange. The gold goes in, you come out. We send in the missile. Big blue bang, and it's all over.'

'Does Fowl know about the bio-bomb?'

'Yep. Knows all about it. Claims he can escape the time-field.'

'That's impossible.'

'Correct.'

'But they'll all be killed!'

'Big deal,' retorted Foaly, and Holly could almost see him shrug. 'That's what you get when you mess with the People.'

Holly was torn. There was no doubt that Fowl was a danger to the civilized underworld. Very few tears would be shed over his body. But the girl, Juliet, she was an innocent. She deserved a chance.

Holly descended to an altitude of two metres. Head height for Butler. The humans had congregated in the wreckage that used to be a hallway. There was disunity between them. The LEP officer could sense it.

Holly glared accusingly at Artemis. 'Have you told them?'

Artemis returned her stare. 'Told them what?'

'Yes, Fairy, told us what?' echoed Juliet belligerently, still a bit miffed over the *mesmer*izing.

'Don't play dumb, Fowl. You know what I'm talking about.'

Artemis never could play dumb for very long. 'Yes, Captain Short. I do. The bio-bomb. Your concern would be touching, if it extended to myself. Nevertheless, do not upset yourself. Everything is proceeding according to plan.'

'According to plan!' gasped Holly, pointing to the

devastation surrounding them. 'Was this part of the plan? And Butler almost getting killed – all part of the plan?'

'No,' Artemis admitted. 'The troll was a slight blip. But irrelevant to the overall scheme.'

Holly resisted the urge to punch the pale human again, turning instead to Butler.

'Listen to reason, for heaven's sake. You cannot escape the time-field. It has never been done.'

Butler's features could have been etched in stone.

'If Artemis says it can be done, then it can.'

'But your sister. Are you willing to risk her life out of loyalty to a felon?'

'Artemis is no felon, miss, he is a genius. Now please remove yourself from my sightline. I am monitoring the main entrance.'

Holly buzzed up to six metres.

'You're crazy. All of you! In five minutes you'll all be dust. Don't you realize?'

Artemis sighed. 'You've had your answer, Captain. Now, please. This is a delicate stage in the proceedings.'

'Proceedings? It's a kidnapping! At least have the guts to call it what it is.'

Artemis's patience was beginning to fray.

'Butler, do we have any tranquillizer hypodermics left?'

The giant manservant nodded, but didn't speak. At that precise moment, if the order came to sedate, he wasn't sure if he would, or could. Luckily Artemis's attention was diverted by activity in the avenue.

'Ah, it would seem the LEP have capitulated. Butler supervise the delivery. But stay alert. Our fairy friends are not above trickery.'

'You're a fine one to talk,' muttered Holly.

Butler hurried to the demolished doorway, checking the load and catch on his Sig Sauer nine-millimetre. He was almost grateful for some military activity to distract him from his dilemma. In situations like these, training took over. There was no room for sentiment.

A fine haze of dust still hung in the air. Butler squinted through it, into the avenue beyond. The fairy filters rigged over his eyes revealed that there were no warm bodies approaching. There was, however, a large trolley seemingly driving itself up to the front door. It was floating on a cushion of shimmering air. Doubtless Master Artemis would have understood the physics of this machine, all Butler cared about was whether or not he could disable it.

The trolley bumped into the first step.

'Automatic compensator, my foot,' snorted Root.

'Yeah, yeah, yeah,' replied Foaly. 'I'm working on it.'

'It's the ransom,' shouted Butler.

Artemis tried to quell the excitement rising in his

chest. This was not the time to allow emotions to enter the equation.

'Check for booby traps.'

Butler stepped cautiously on to the porch. Shards of disintegrated gargoyle lay scattered beneath his feet.

'No hostiles. Seems to be self-propelled.'

The trolley lurched over the steps.

'I don't know who's driving this thing, but he could do with a few lessons.'

Butler bent low to the ground, scanning the trolley's underside.

'No explosive devices visible.'

He extracted a Sweeper from his pocket, extending the telescopic aerial.

'No bugs either. Nothing detectable at any rate. But what do we have here?'

'Uh oh,' said Foaly.

'It's a camera.'

Butler reached in, pulling the fish-eye lens out by the cable.

'Nighty-night, gentlemen.'

In spite of the load it carried, the trolley responded easily to Butler's touch, gliding across the threshold into the lobby. It stood there humming softly, as though waiting to be unloaded.

Now that the moment had come, Artemis was almost afraid to seize it. It was hard to believe that after all these months, his wicked scheme was minutes away from fruition. Of course these last few minutes were the vital ones, and the most dangerous.

'Open it,' he said at last, surprised at the tremble in his own voice.

It was an irresistible instant. Juliet approached tentatively, spangled eyes wide. Even Holly closed the throttle a notch, dropping until her feet brushed the marble tiling. Butler unzipped the black tarpaulin, dragging it back across the cargo.

Nobody said a thing. Artemis imagined that somewhere the *1812 Overture* was playing. The gold sat there, stacked in shining rows. It seemed to have an aura, a warmth, but also an inherent danger. There were a lot of people willing to die or kill for the unimaginable wealth this gold could bring.

Holly was mesmerized. Fairies have an affinity for minerals, they are of the earth. But gold was their favourite. Its lustre. Its allure.

'They paid,' she breathed. 'I can't believe it.'

'Neither can I,' murmured Artemis. 'Butler, is it real?'

Butler hefted a bar from the stack. He dug the tip of a throwing knife into the ingot, gouging out a small sliver.

'It's real all right,' he said, holding the scraping up to the light. 'This one, at any rate.'

'Good. Very good. Begin unloading it, would you? We'll send the trolley back out with Captain Short.'

Hearing her name dispelled Holly's gold fever.

'Artemis, give it up. No human has ever succeeded in keeping fairy gold. And they've been trying for centuries. The LEP will do anything to protect their property.'

Artemis shook his head. Amused.

'I've told you …'

Holly took him by the shoulders. 'You cannot escape! Don't you understand?'

The boy returned her gaze coolly.

'I can escape, Holly. Look in my eyes and tell me that I can't.'

So she did. Captain Holly Short gazed into her captor's blue-black eyes and she saw the truth in there. And for a moment she believed it.

'There's still time,' she said desperately. 'There must be something. I have magic.'

A crease of annoyance wrinkled the boy's brow.

'I hate to disappoint you, Captain, but there is absolutely nothing.'

Artemis paused, his gaze tugged momentarily upstairs to the converted loft. Perhaps, he thought. Do I really need all this gold? And was his conscience not pricking him, leeching the sweetness from his victory? He shook himself. Stick to the plan. Stick to the plan. No emotion.

Artemis felt a familiar hand on his shoulder.

'Everything all right?'

'Yes, Butler. Keep unloading. Get Juliet to help. I need to talk to Captain Short.'

'Are you sure there's nothing wrong?'

Artemis sighed. 'No, old friend, I'm not sure. But it's too late now.'

Butler nodded, returning to his task. Juliet toddled along behind him like a terrier.

'Now, Captain. About your magic.'

'What about it?' Holly's eyes were hooded with suspicion.

'What would I have to do to buy a wish?'

Holly glanced at the trolley. 'Well, that depends. What do you have to bargain with?'

Root was not what you'd call relaxed. Increasingly wide bands of yellow light were poking through the blue. Minutes left. Minutes. His migraine was not helped by the pungent cigar feeding toxins into his system.

'Have all non-essential personnel been evacuated?'

'Unless they've sneaked back in since the last time you asked me.'

'Not now, Foaly. Believe me, now is not the time. Anything from Captain Short?'

'Nope. We lost video after the troll thing. I'd guess the battery is ruptured. We'd better get that helmet off her ASAP, or the radiation will fry her brain. That'd be a pity after all this work.'

Foaly returned to his console. A red light began pulsing gently.

'Wait, motion sensor. We've got activity by the main entrance.'

Root crossed to the screens. 'Can you enhance it?'

'No problem.' Foaly punched in the coordinates, blowing it up 400 per cent.

Root sat down on the nearest chair.

'Am I seeing what I think I'm seeing?'

'You sure are.' Foaly chuckled. 'This is even better than the suit of armour.'

Holly was coming out. With the gold.

Retrieval were on her in half a second.

'Let's get you out of the danger zone, Captain,' urged a sprite, catching Holly by the elbow.

Another ran a rad-sensor over her helmet.

'We've got a power source breach here, Captain. We need to get your head sprayed immediately.'

Holly opened her mouth to protest, and had it instantly filled with rad-suppressant foam.

'Can't this wait?' she spluttered.

'Sorry, Captain. Time is of the essence. The commander wants a debriefing before we detonate.'

Holly was rushed towards the Mobile Ops unit, her feet barely touching the ground. All around her Retrieval

Cleaners scanned the grounds for any trace of the siege. Techies dismantled the field dishes, making ready to pull the plug. Grunts steered the trolley towards the portal. It was imperative that everything be relocated to a safe distance before the bio-bomb went in.

Root was waiting on the steps.

'Holly,' he blurted. 'I mean Captain. You made it.'

'Yessir. Thank you, sir.'

'And the gold too. This is a real feather in your cap.'

'Well, not all, Commander. About half I think.'

Root nodded. 'No matter. We'll have the rest soon enough.'

Holly wiped rad-foam from her brow.

'I've been thinking about that, sir. Fowl made another mistake. He never ordered me not to re-enter the house, and seeing as he brought me in there in the first place, the invitation still stands. I could go in and mind-wipe the occupants. We could hide the gold in the walls and do another time-stop tomorrow night ...'

'No, Captain.'

'But, sir ...'

Root's features regained whatever tension they'd lost.

'No, Captain. The Council is not about to hold off for some kidnapping Mud Man. It's just not going to happen. I have my orders, and believe me they're written in stone.'

Holly trailed Root into the mobile.

'But the girl, sir. She's an innocent!'

'Casualty of war. She threw her lot in with the wrong side. Nothing can be done for her now.'

Holly was incredulous. 'A casualty of war? How can you say that? A life is a life.'

Root spun sharply, grasping her by the shoulders.

'You did what you could, Holly,' he said. 'No one could have done more. You even retrieved most of the ransom. You're suffering from what humans call Stockholm Syndrome: you have bonded with your captors. Don't worry, it will pass. But those people in there, they know. About us. Nothing can save them now.'

Foaly looked up from his calculations.

'Not true. Technically. Welcome back, by the way.'

Holly couldn't spare even a second to return the greeting.

'What do you mean not true?'

'I'm fine, seeing as you asked.'

'Foaly!' shouted Root and Holly in unison.

'Well, like the Book says, "If the Mud Man gold can gather, In spite of magick or fairy glamour, Then that gold is his to keep, Until he lies in eternal sleep." So if he lives, he wins. It's that simple. Not even the Council will go against the Book.'

Root scratched his chin. 'Should I be worried?'

Foaly laughed mirthlessly. 'No. Those guys are as good as dead.'

'As good as isn't good enough.'

'Is that an order?'

'Affirmative, soldier.'

'I'm not a soldier,' said Foaly, and pressed the button.

Butler was more than a little surprised.

'You gave it back?'

Artemis nodded. 'About half. We still have quite a nest egg. About fifteen million dollars at today's market prices.'

Butler usually wouldn't ask. But this time he had to. 'Why, Artemis? Can you tell me?'

'I suppose so.' The boy smiled. 'I felt we owed the captain something. For services rendered.'

'Is that all?'

Artemis nodded. No need to talk about the wish. It could be perceived as weakness.

'Hmm,' said Butler, smarter than he looked.

'Now, we should celebrate,' enthused Artemis, deftly changing the subject. 'Some champagne, I think.'

The boy strode to the kitchen before Butler's gaze could dissect him.

By the time the others caught up, Artemis had already filled three glasses with Dom Perignon.

'I'm a minor, I know, but I'm sure Mother wouldn't mind. Just this once.'

Butler felt that something was afoot. Nevertheless, he took the crystal flute offered to him.

Juliet looked at her big brother.

'Is this OK?'

'I suppose so.' He took a breath. 'You know I love you, don't you, sis?'

Juliet scowled — something else that the local louts found very endearing. She smacked her brother on the shoulder.

'You're so emotional for a bodyguard.'

Butler looked his employer straight in the eye.

'You want us to drink this, don't you, Artemis?'

Artemis met his gaze squarely. 'Yes, Butler. I do.'

Without another word Butler drained his glass, Juliet followed suit. The manservant tasted the tranquillizer immediately, and although he would have had ample time to snap Artemis Fowl's neck, he didn't. No need for Juliet to be distressed in her final moments.

Artemis watched his friends sink to the floor. A pity to deceive them. But if they had been alerted to the plan, their anxiety could have counteracted the sedative. He gazed at the bubbles swirling in his own glass. Time for the most audacious step in his scheme. With only the barest hint of hesitation, he swallowed the tranquillizer-laced champagne.

Artemis waited calmly for the drug to take hold of his system. He didn't have to wait long, for each dose had been calculated according to body weight. As his thoughts began to swirl, it occurred to him that he might never awaken again. It's a bit late for doubts, he chided himself, and sank into unconsciousness.

'She's away,' said Foaly, leaning back from the console. 'It's out of my hands now.'

They followed the missile's progress through polarized windows. It really was a remarkable piece of equipment. Because its main weapon was light, the fallout could be focused to an exact radius. The radioactive element used in the core was solinium 2, which had a half-life of fourteen seconds. This effectively meant that Foaly could tune the bio-bomb to blue-rinse only Fowl Manor and not one blade of grass more, plus the building would be radiation-free in under a minute. In the event that a few solinium flares refused to be focused, they would be contained by the time-field. Murder made easy.

'The flight path is pre-programmed,' explained Foaly, though no one was paying a blind bit of attention. 'She'll sail into the lobby and detonate. The casing and firing mechanism are plastic alloy and will completely disintegrate. Clean as a whistle.'

Root and Holly followed the bomb's arc. As predicted, it swooped through the decimated doorway without knocking so much as a sliver of stone from the medieval walls. Holly switched her attention to the missile's nose-cam. For a moment she caught a glimpse of the grand hallway where she had, until recently, been a prisoner. It was empty. Not a human in sight. Maybe, she thought. Just maybe. Then she looked at Foaly and the technology at his fingertips. And she realized that the humans were as good as dead.

The bio-bomb detonated. A blue orb of condensed light crackled and spread, filling every corner of the manor with its deadly rays. Flowers withered, insects shrivelled and fish died in their tanks. Not one cubic millimetre was spared. Artemis Fowl and his cohorts could not have escaped. It was impossible.

Holly sighed, turning away from the already dwindling blue-rinse. For all his grand designs, Artemis had been a mere mortal in the end. And for some reason she mourned his passing.

Root was more pragmatic. 'OK. Suit up. Full blackout gear.'

'It's perfectly safe,' said Foaly. 'Didn't you ever listen in school?'

The commander snorted. 'I trust science about as far as I could throw you, Foaly. Radiation has a habit of hanging around when certain *scientists* have assured us it has dissipated. No one steps outside the unit without blackout gear. So that counts you out, Foaly. Only bipedal suits. Anyway I want you on monitors, just in case ...'

In case of what? wondered Foaly, but he didn't comment. Save it for an *I told you so* later.

Root turned to Holly.

•𖤐𖧵)𖣔•𖤐𖩤•𖤐•𖣐𖦿𖤐𖦿•𖤐𖨒𖧵)𖦿•𖤐𖧵𖦿𖧵

'Are you ready, Captain?'

Going back in. The idea of identifying three cadavers didn't appeal to Holly. But she knew it was her duty. She was the only one with first-hand knowledge of the interior.

'Yessir. On my way.'

Holly selected a blackout suit from the rack, pulling it on over her jumpsuit. As per training, she checked the gauge before tugging the vulcanized cowl. A dip in pressure would indicate a rip, which could prove fatal in the long term.

Root lined up the insertion team at the perimeter. The remains of Retrieval One were about as eager to insert themselves into the manor as they would be to juggle Atlantean stink balloons.

'You're certain the big one is gone?'

'Yes, Captain Kelp. He's gone, one way or another.'

Trouble wasn't convinced. 'Because that's one mean human. I think he has magic of his own.'

Corporal Grub giggled, and got an immediate clip on the ear for himself. He muttered something about telling Mummy and quickly strapped on his helmet.

Root felt his complexion redden. 'Let's move out. Your mission is to locate and recover the bullion. Watch for booby traps. I didn't trust Fowl when he was alive, and I definitely don't trust him now that he's dead.'

The phrase 'booby traps' got everyone's attention. The

idea of a Bouncing Betty anti-personnel mine exploding at head height was enough to dispel any nonchalance in the troops. No one built weapons of cruelty like the Mud Men.

As the junior Recon officer, Holly was on point. And even though there weren't supposed to be any hostiles in the manor, she found her gun hand automatically straying to the Neutrino 2000.

The mansion was eerily quiet, with only the fizzle of the last few solinium flares to alleviate the stillness. Death was there too, in the silence. The manor was a cradle of death. Holly could smell it. Behind those medieval walls lay the bodies of a million insects, and under its floors the cooling corpses of spiders and mice.

They approached the doorway tentatively. Holly swept the area with an X-ray scanner. Nothing under the flagstones but dirt, and a nest of dead money-spiders.

'Clear,' she said into her microphone. 'I'm going in. Foaly, have you got your ears on?'

'I'm right there with you, darlin',' replied the centaur. 'Unless you step on a landmine, in which case I'm way back in the Operations Room.'

'Are you getting any thermals?'

'Not after a blue-rinse. We have residual heat signatures all over the place. Mostly solinium flares. It won't calm down for a couple of days.'

'But no radiation, right?'

'That's right.'

Root snorted in disbelief. Over the headsets it sounded like an elephant sneezing.

'It looks like we're going to have to sweep this house the old-fashioned way,' he grumbled.

'Make it quick,' advised Foaly. 'I give it five minutes tops before Fowl Manor rejoins the world at large.'

Holly stepped through what used to be the doorway. The chandelier swung gently from the concussive force of the missile's detonation, but otherwise everything was as she remembered it.

'The gold is downstairs. In my cell.'

Nobody answered. Not in words. Someone did manage a retch. Right into the microphone. Holly spun around. Trouble was doubled over, clutching his stomach.

'I don' feel so good,' he groaned. A tad unnecessarily, considering the pool of vomit all over his boots.

Corporal Grub took a breath, possibly to utter a sentence containing the word *Mummy*. What came out was a jet of concentrated bile. Unfortunately Grub didn't have the opportunity to open his visor before the illness struck. It was not a pretty sight.

'Ugh,' said Holly, pressing the corporal's visor-release button. A tsunami of regurgitated rations flooded over Grub's blackout suit.

'Oh, for heaven's sake,' muttered Root, elbowing past the brothers. He didn't get very far. One step over the threshold and he was throwing up with the rest of them.

Holly pointed her helmet-cam at the stricken officers.

'What the hell is going on here, Foaly?'

'I'm searching. Hold on.'

Holly could hear computer keys being punched furiously.

'OK. Sudden vomiting. Spatial nausea … Oh no.'

'What?' asked Holly. But she already knew. Maybe she always had.

'It's the magic,' blurted Foaly, words barely decipherable in his excitement. 'They can't enter the house until Fowl is dead. It's like an extreme allergic reaction. That means, unbelievable, that means …'

'They made it,' completed Holly. 'He's alive. Artemis Fowl is alive.'

'D'Arvit,' groaned Root, and heaved another quart of vomit on to the terracotta tiles.

Holly went on alone. She had to see for herself. If Fowl's corpse was here, it would be with the gold, of that she was certain.

The same family portraits glared down at her, but now they seemed smug rather than austere. Holly was tempted to loose a few blasts into them from the Neutrino 2000. But that would be against the rules. If Artemis Fowl had beaten them, then that was it. There would be no recriminations.

She descended the stairway to her cell. The door was still swinging slightly from the bio-bomb concussion. A solinium flare ricocheted around the room like a trapped bolt of blue lightning. Holly stepped inside, half-afraid of what she might or might not see.

There was nothing. Nothing dead at any rate. Just gold. Two hundred ingots approximately. Piled on the mattress of her cot. Nice neat military rows. Good old Butler, the only human ever to take on a troll and win.

'Commander? Are you receiving? Over.'

'Affirmative, Captain. Body count?'

'Negative on the bodies, sir. I found the rest of the ransom.'

There was along silence.

'Leave it, Holly. You know the rules. We're pulling out.'

'But, sir. There must be a way ...'

Foaly broke in on the conversation. 'But nothing, Captain. I'm counting down the seconds until daylight here, and I don't like our odds if we have to exit at high noon.'

Holly sighed. It made sense. The People could chose their exit time, as long as they left before the field disintegrated. It just galled her to think they'd been beaten by a human. An adolescent human at that.

She took a last look around the cell. A big ball of hatred had been born here, she realized, and it would have to be dealt with sooner or later. Holly jammed her pistol back into its holster. Preferably sooner. Fowl was the winner this time, but someone like him wouldn't be able to rest on his laurels. He would be back with some other moneymaking scheme. And when he arrived, he would find Holly Short waiting for him. Waiting with a big gun and a smile.

The ground was soft by the time-stop perimeter. Half a millennium's bad drainage from the medieval walls had transformed the foundations into a virtual bog. So that was where Mulch surfaced.

The soft ground wasn't the only reason for choosing that exact spot. The other reason was the smell. A good tunnel dwarf can pick up the scent of gold through half a kilometre of granite bedrock. Mulch Diggums had one of the best noses in the business.

The hovertrolley floated virtually unguarded. Two of Retrieval's finest were stationed beside the recovered ransom, but at the moment they were having a little giggle at their stricken commander.

''E can't half chuck it, can't 'e, Chix?'

Chix nodded, mimicking Root's spewing technique.

Chix Verbil's pantomime antics provided the perfect cover for a spot of pilfering. Mulch gave his tubes a clearing before clambering from the tunnel. The last thing he needed was for a sudden burst of gas to alert the LEP to his presence. He needn't have worried. He could have slapped Chix Verbil in the face with a wet stink-worm and the sprite wouldn't have noticed.

In a matter of seconds, he had transferred two dozen ingots into the tunnel. It was the easiest job he had ever pulled. Mulch had to stifle a giggle as he dropped the last two bars down the hole. Julius had really done him a favour, getting him involved in this whole affair. Things couldn't have worked out much better. He was free as a bird, rich and, best of all, presumed dead. By the time the LEP realized that the gold was missing, Mulch Diggums would be half a continent away. If they realized at all.

The dwarf lowered himself into the ground. It would take several trips to move his treasure trove, but it would be worth the delay. With this kind of money, he could take early retirement. He would have to completely disappear of course, but a plan was already forming in his devious mind.

He would live above ground for a spell. Masquerade as a human dwarf, with an aversion to light. Perhaps buy a penthouse with thick blinds. In Manhattan perhaps, or Monte Carlo. It might seem odd, of course, a dwarf shutting himself away from the sun. But then again, he would be an obscenely rich dwarf. And humans will accept any story, however outlandish, when there's something in it for them. Preferably something green that folds.

*

272

Artemis could hear a voice calling his name. There was a face behind the voice, but it was blurred, hard to make out. His father perhaps?

'Father?' The word was strange in his mouth. Unused. Rusty. Artemis opened his eyes.

Butler was leaning over him.

'Artemis. You're awake.'

'Ah, Butler. It's you.'

Artemis got to his feet, head spinning with the effort. He expected Butler's hand at his elbow to steady him. It didn't come. Juliet was lying on a chaise longue, dribbling on to the cushions. Obviously the draft hadn't worn off yet.

'It was just sleeping pills, Butler. Harmless.'

The manservant's eyes had a dangerous glint. 'Explain yourself.'

Artemis rubbed his eyes. 'Later, Butler. I'm feeling a bit –'

Butler stepped into his path. 'Artemis, my sister is lying drugged on that couch. She was almost killed. So explain yourself now!'

Artemis realized that he'd been given an order. He considered being offended, then decided that perhaps Butler was right. He had gone too far.

'I didn't tell you about the sleeping pills because you'd fight them. It's only natural. And it was imperative to the plan that we all go to sleep immediately.'

'The plan?'

Artemis lowered himself into a comfortable chair.

'The time-field was the key to this whole affair. It's the LEP's ace in the hole. It's what has made them unbeatable for all these years. Any incident can be contained. That and the bio-bomb make a formidable combination.'

'So why did we have to be drugged?'

Artemis smiled. 'Look out of the window. Don't you see? They're gone. It's over.'

Butler glanced through the net curtains. The light was bright and clear. Not a hint of blue. Nevertheless, the manservant was unimpressed. 'They're gone for now. They'll be back tonight, I guarantee it.'

'No. That's against the rules. We beat them. That's it, game over.'

Butler raised an eyebrow. 'The sleeping pills, Artemis?'

'Not to be distracted, I see.'

Butler's answer was an implacable silence.

'The sleeping pills. Very well. I had to think of a way to escape the time-field. I trawled through the Book, but there was nothing. Not a clue. The People themselves have not yet developed a way. So I went back to their Old Testament, back to when their lives and ours were intertwined. You know the stories: elves that made shoes during the night, sprites that cleaned houses. Back when we coexisted to a certain extent. Magical favours in exchange for their fairy forts. The big

274

one, of course, was Santa Claus.'

Butler's eyebrows nearly jumped off the front of his face.

'Santa Claus?'

Artemis raised his palms. 'I know, I know. I was a tad sceptical myself. But apparently our little corporate-image Santa Claus is not descended from a Turkish saint, he is a shadow of San D'Klass, the third king of the Frond Elfin dynasty. He is known as San the Deluded.'

'Not a great title, as titles go.'

'Admittedly. D'Klass thought that the greed of the Mud People in his kingdom could be assuaged by distributing lavish gifts. He would marshal all the great wizards once a year and have them throw up a great time-stop over vast regions. Flocks of sprites would be sent out to deliver the presents while the humans were asleep. Of course, it didn't work. Human greed can never be assuaged, especially not by gifts.'

Butler frowned. 'What if the humans … we, that is … What if we had woken up?'

'Ah yes. Excellent question. The heart of the matter. We wouldn't wake up. That is the nature of the time-stop. Whatever your state of consciousness going in, that's how you stay. You can neither wake up nor fall asleep. You must have noticed the fatigue in your bones these last few hours, yet your mind would not let you sleep.'

Butler nodded. Things were getting clearer, in a

roundabout sort of way.

'So my theory was that the only way to escape the time-field was to simply fall asleep. Our own consciousness was all that kept us imprisoned.'

'You risked an awful lot on a theory, Artemis.'

'Not just a theory. We did have a test subject.'

'Who? Ah, Angeline.'

'Yes. My mother. Because of her narcotic-induced slumber, she moved with the natural order of time, unhindered by the time-field. If she had not, I would have simply surrendered to the LEP and submitted to their mind wipe.'

Butler snorted. He doubted it.

'So, because we could not fall asleep naturally, I simply administered us all a dose of Mother's pills. Simple.'

'You cut it pretty fine though. Another minute ...'

'Agreed.' The boy nodded. 'Things were tense there at the end. It was necessary in order to double-bluff the LEP.'

He paused so that Butler could process the information.

'Well, am I forgiven?'

Butler sighed. On the chaise lounge, Juliet snored like a drunken sailor. He smiled suddenly.

'Yes, Artemis. All is forgiven. Just one thing ...'

'Yes?'

'Never again. Fairies are too ... human.'

'You're right,' said Artemis, the crow's feet deepening around his eyes. 'Never again. We shall restrict ourselves to more tasteful ventures in the future. Legal, I can't promise.'

Butler nodded. It was close enough.

'Now, young Master, shouldn't we check on your mother?'

Artemis grew paler, if that were possible. Could the captain have reneged on her promise? She would certainly be entitled to.

'Yes. I suppose we should. Let Juliet rest. She's earned it.'

He cast his eyes upwards, along the stairs. It had been too much to hope for that he could trust the fairy. After all, he had held her captive against her will. He berated himself silently. Imagine parting with all those millions for the promise of a wish. Oh, the gullibility.

Then the loft door opened.

Butler drew his weapon instantly.

'Artemis, behind me. Intruders.'

The boy waved him away. 'No, Butler. I don't think so.'

His heart pounded in his ears, blood pulsed in his fingertips. Could it be? Could it possibly be? A figure appeared on the stairs. Wraith-like in a towelled robe, her hair wet from the shower.

'Arty?' she called. 'Arty, are you there?'

Artemis wanted to answer, he wanted to race up the

grand stairway, arms outstretched. But he couldn't. His cerebral functions had deserted him.

Angeline Fowl descended, one hand resting lightly on the banister. Artemis had forgotten how graceful his mother was. Her bare feet skipped over the carpeted steps and soon she was standing before him.

'Morning, darling,' she said brightly, as though it were just another day.

''M-Mother,' stammered Artemis.

'Well, give me a hug.'

Artemis stepped into his mother's embrace. It was warm and strong. She was wearing perfume. He felt like the boy he was.

'I'm sorry, Arty,' she whispered into his ear.

'Sorry for what?'

'For everything. For the last few months, I haven't been myself. But things are going to change. Time to stop living in the past.'

Artemis felt a tear on his cheek. He wasn't sure whose tear it was.

'And I don't have a present for you.'

'A present?' said Artemis.

'Of course,' sang his mother, spinning him around. 'Don't you know what day it is?'

'Day?'

'It's Christmas Day, you silly boy. Christmas Day! Presents are traditional, are they not?'

•ᑌᗩᗷᕮᑎ᙭⊕ᗪ᙭⊕ᗝᗩᗷ᙮• ᗷᗩᗝ•

Yes, thought Artemis. Traditional. San D'Klass.

'And look at this place. Drab as a mausoleum. Butler?'

The manservant hurriedly pocketed his Sig Sauer.

'Yes, ma'am?'

'Get on the phone to Brown Thomas. The platinum set number. Reopen my account. Tell Hélène I want a Yuletide makeover. The works.'

'Yes, ma'am. The works.'

'Oh, and wake up Juliet. I want my things moved into the main bedroom. That attic is far too dusty.'

'Yes, ma'am. Right away, ma'am.'

Angeline Fowl linked her son's arm.

'Now, Arty, I want to know everything. First of all, what happened here?'

'Remodelling,' said Artemis. 'The old doorway was riddled with damp.'

Angeline frowned, completely unconvinced. 'I see. And how about school? Have you decided on a career?'

While his mouth answered these everyday questions, Artemis's mind was in turmoil. He was a boy again. His life was going to change utterly. His plans would have to be much more devious than usual if they were to escape his mother's attention. But it would be worth it.

Angeline Fowl was wrong. She had brought him a Christmas present.

EPILOGUE

Now that you have reviewed the case file, you must realize what a dangerous creature this Fowl is.

There is a tendency to romanticize Artemis. To attribute to him qualities that he does not possess. The fact that he used his wish to heal his mother is not a sign of affection. He did it simply because the Social Services were already investigating his case, and it was only a matter of time before he was put into care.

He kept the existence of the People quiet only so that he could continue to exploit them over the years, which he did on several occasions. His one mistake was leaving Captain Short alive. Holly became the LEP's foremost expert in the Artemis Fowl cases, and was invaluable in the fight against the People's most feared enemy. This fight was to continue across several decades.

Ironically, the greatest triumph for both protagonists was the time they were forced to cooperate during the goblin insurgence. But that's another story.

Report compiled by: Doctor J. Argon, B.Psych, for the LEP Academy files.
Details are 94 per cent accurate, 6 per cent unavoidable extrapolation.

<u>The End</u>